Thomas Smith

The Heart's Chronicles

A Poem

Thomas Smith

The Heart's Chronicles
A Poem

ISBN/EAN: 9783337158446

Printed in Europe, USA, Canada, Australia, Japan

Cover: Foto ©Andreas Hilbeck / pixelio.de

More available books at **www.hansebooks.com**

The Heart's Chronicle,

AND MISCELLANEOUS PIECES.

THE

HEART'S CHRONICLE:

A POEM,

IN THREE BOOKS OR PARTS.

WITH

Miscellaneous Pieces.

By THOMAS SMITH.

A SEQUEL TO THE VOLUME PRINTED IN 1867.

London :

J. SUCH, TYP., 3, OLD FISH STREET, DOCTORS' COMMONS.

—

1873.

NOTE.

The edition of this book being (like the last) a very limited one, friends are enjoined not to expect that a second copy can be supplied in the event of the presentation copy being lost.

CONTENTS.

PREFACE.

WHEN my book was printed in 1867, to which this is intended as a sequel, it was explained in the Preface that it was principally done in performance of an early promise made to my mother (then the custodian of my writings from boyhood), on condition of my being allowed to discriminate which should be preserved and which destroyed; and partly that I might include some subsequent things in my own possession, rather crowding my space, and that thus, in a certain sense and in an unobtrusive form, I might set my literary " house in order."

A recent bereavement (perhaps the most severe that any man, especially one in middle life can sustain)—the loss of my wife in December, 1871—compelled me to endeavour to find some little resource against the gloom of the period *by occupation*, such as I confess I have always found to yield consolation in the darkest hours, and by which many a trouble has been alleviated through the intervention of the only true healer of mental wounds — Time ; and I, therefore, present this book as indicating again, and more in the meaning of the prophet's words, the intention of setting my " house in order."

" The Heart's Chronicle " was nearly completed when I entered upon the task I had imposed upon myself; and after I had put the finishing lines to the MS. and collected my miscellaneous pieces (destroying fragments which had been left for a more convenient season), many things occurred to call forth little compositions which the reader will observe in the later miscellanies. I found I had then sufficient " copy " (to use a technical phrase,) to form the volume now presented ; and, as many of the pieces were already in the hands of those to whom they were originally and severally addressed, I consulted my friend-critic and printer (as set forth in the lines at the end, entitled " The Typiad,") and hence the result.

The previous book having been printed

"for private circulation only," this, of course, as a sequel, is also issued to friends, and especially to those who have retained a copy of the other. Still, had I been disposed to publish for general reading, and thus to have entered an arena where there are already too many unknown writers, perhaps I should not have received the discouragement that might have been intended by *harsh criticism;* for I do not forget the *compliments in this way* which are, and have been, paid even to splendid genius and acknowledged worth. I thus *might* have flattered myself that such ungenial criticism was worth little more or less than the unqualified praise of too-partial friends, and that both, having equal right to their opinions, might mutually have erred. I would prefer, therefore, to say, in all humility, to either friend or critic, I hope there may be found a few things which may redeem many shortcomings, and shall seem to kindly eyes as "a little leaven which leaveneth the whole."

T. S.

THE
HEART'S CHRONICLE.

PART FIRST.

THE HEART'S CHRONICLE.

ARGUMENT.

The Poem opens with an invocation to the Spirit of Song, to inspire the Muse with a vision of the human heart, symbolised as a sphere or an aggregation of realms synonymous with the Passions. The Spirit of the Heart hears the call, and in rebuking language points out some of the attributes and peculiarities of the heart, but eventually acceding to the desire of the Muse, a chorus of attendant spirits concludes the First Part.

THE HEART'S CHRONICLE.

PART FIRST.

Sing Muse!—unfetter'd by a spellbound dream,
Thy lyre awake! and breathe a wonderous theme;
Behold the vassal-planet of the soul,
To whose behest the passions own control!
The soul the sun—the heart the planet true—
Whose vast domains are opening to my view.
Fix'd in the orbit trac'd by power on high,
Nurtur'd by love, and joys that never die;
But, oft convuls'd by mortal throes and strife,
'Midst dismal shades that veil the sun of life,
It burns with hate, and dares the desperate path
That danger spreads before its stormy wrath;
It trembling quails before an unseen fear,
And halts with doubt, upon its grand career;

B

Or fill'd with love, it utters spirit-prayer
To mortal ears unmindful of its care;
Or wrapt in dreams, no waking hours destroy,
Sails a light bark on summer seas of joy;
Melodious songs, or ponderous choral sounds
Rise from its groves, or thunder from its bounds;
'Neath genial suns it ripens with the years,
Calm'd and refresh'd with plenitude of tears.
A world itself, with varying lands replete,
Where teeming harvests every climate meet.
Sing Muse this realm!—its thousand monarchs sing!
Apollo tunes thy lyre on every string.
  Why silent thus? doth no responsive chord
Bid drowsy nature breathe a living word?
Spirit of Song! O let me hear thy tone,
My soul is gazing upward to thy throne,
Give me to see this heart-world and its powers,
Climb its rude landscapes—cull its sweetest flowers.
Hide not thy face, awake the morning beam,
And wrap my spirit in a mystic dream.
Yet winds are still—and sleep in odorous rest,
By Flora crown'd with trophies from her breast.
I taste the sweetness of mysterious air,
And spellbound-fancy seems a chain to wear;
Constrain'd mine eyes are wrapt in darkness dire,
Night reigns supreme, nor yields to orient fire.

O let me see the purpling eastern skies ;—
Let gradual morn beams charm my waking eyes,
E'en though commanded to attune my lay
When first my vision hails the ruddy day,
I pant to leave Cimmerian shades of night,
And dare the perils of poetic flight.
Then lead thy train, O moon of night away,
And thou, bright Hesperus, pale before the day
Let shadowy spells no more oppress my brain
But bright Apollo's lyre inspire the strain.
The sun of morning teach my night-bound eyes
Where is the orient,—where poetic skies.
  'Tis the souls' sabbath ! yet a voice I hear
In tones rebuking pride, yet chiding fear,
I rest supremely from life's coming cares
Yet court the day with every task it bears.
Still do I hear the words which hold my soul
Bound to their import, and occult control.
Whilst to my call a spirit voice responds,
And with its accents bursts my chafing bonds.
Thus as it speaks, my startled listening ears
Receive the words, as from celestial spheres ;
The solemn voice, unwilling to deny,
Thus to my restless muse gives forth reply.—
    " What wouldst thou know ? what none of all
        thy kind

" Hath e'er confronted or shall e'er attain?
" The human Heart! emotion's battle ground
" Since Adam lost his holy heritage—
" And Eden with its crystal walls o'erthrown
" Remain'd no more the Angel's trysting place;
" Whence flow the passions, and from sources deep
" For ever rise, the primal forms occult
" That may hereafter vanquish e'en the soul.
" Not that ethereal height—the throne of God
" Dar'd fallen Angels to attempt to seize,
" But in the nature of the primal curse—
" This realm,—the human heart, became convuls'd
" With all the conflict of contending foes,
" And thence it needs fair guidance to behold
" Its heights—its depths, and all its mysteries.
    " Hast thou not seen on ancient record plac'd
" The prophet-words in characters of fire,
" Spoken by him of Anathoth—who saith
" ' The heart deceitful is above all things
" ' And wicked desperately; who shall know?'
" ' Yet doth the heart from its own fulness yield
" Evil and good '—the Lord of Sabbath said
" When hungry followers pluck'd the yellow corn.
" Thus far thou knowest, and should'st be content
" With teachings such as holy records yield.
    " Thy gaze avert—too far beyond thy power

" Thou seek'st to trace the things thou soon shalt
    know,
" But not in mortal garb. Now should'st thou
    pause
" And in thy search for knowledge thou may'st learn
" What most befits thee in thy present hour.
    " The glorious orb thou seest, it is the soul,
" The spirit-essence of created man
" That dwells in ether, and whose fount of life
" Is ever rising from celestial springs
" O'erflowing nectar, and the food of gods—
" Ambrosia. Mortal never can attain
" That realm of light whilst trammell'd in his clay;
" So circumscribe th view, and closer draw
" Thine eyes towards the earth thou dwell'st upon,
" And midway, see a world thou hast o'erlook'd
" In thy too eager longing. Pois'd between
" The mortal and immortal, see it glows
" With nascent fires; and songs and choral strains
" Whilst ever rising are for ever new.
" It is the vassal sphere that serves the soul,
" Prompts all its prayers, its sorrows and its hopes,
" But, stands between the things of time and sense
" Sole arbiter, whose fiat rules supreme.
    " Then mortal know that in this pilgrimage
" Thou see'st with vision strengthen'd, and awhile

" Must list and marvel. I will show some things
" I may entrust thy senses with, and tell
" Thine own conceited heart some bitter truths.
" Ne'er yet was one whole, perfect heart in man;
" Even the holy Nazarene, to prove
" How truly mortal nature dwelt in him,
" Twice to despair gave momentary space.
   " Thou feel'st a breezy influence arise
" That moves thee onward—prompts thy eagerness ;
" Thou heed'st it not but as a summer wind
" That bloweth where it listeth. Thou shalt know
" It is the breath of change,—Time's myrmidon,
" That worketh ever in his silent path,
" And with mutation baffles all control.
   " Full oft Titania doth complain that she,
" Her court, her revels, and her reign disturb'd
" By mortal sounds within her fairy haunts,
" Hath sought in far recesses, time to time,
" Deep sylvan shades, remote from human ken ;
" That yet the approaching hum—and onward
    march
" Of gath'ring peoples, adverse to her sports
" Seem to pursue her. But she doth forget
" That in long tracts of time—primeval days
" When Earth was young—where she doth seek to
    hold

" In deepest shades the frolics of her court,
" The sons of men then held it as their own,
" Whilst she did revel where the cities are,
" To change with Time's mutations as they roll.
" In you deep valley's bosom calmly sleeps
" The Lake of Tears,—subsidence of the heart ;
" A thousand tributary streams convey
" Their rippling wavelets to the silent spring;
" Then when the o'ercharg'd passion breaks its
    bound,
" Lo ! from the conduits of the aching eyes
" Pour forth the soothing solace o'er domains
" Of sorrow and despair.   A tiny stream
" Is from the heights of pleasure sometimes forc'd,
" And thus the tears of joy will kindly blend,
" To sweeten the surrounding bitterness.
" And often too the scalding tears that flow
" To memory's vales are from hope's hilltops drawn,
" And but for faithful eyelids gushing forth,
" Would burst the bondage of the fetter'd heart.
" Or when by deep despair, and sudden wrong,
" The lake is spell-bound,—frozen at its source !
" The callous heart gives then no outward sign ;
" Like weeping Niobe—the tears that fall
" Come from a stony statue grief hath made
" And change to petrifaction all the heart.

" Now cautiously survey the rising slopes
" That all surround this reservoir of tears,
" And lead away up to the level plain
" And far beyond. Stretch'd forth in boundless view
" The misty mountains of the lands of pride
" Rise toward heaven and mimic god-like strength.
" But oft when storms and tempests tear the heart,
" Or the full orb of heaven too fiercely beams,
" Their unreal substance melts before the sun
" Or crumbles 'neath the bitter winds of truth ;
" But hope's pure hills stand sun-bright in their
        health
" Unchang'd by bitter storms.   Bas'd on a rock
" Their verdure blossoms through the mortal year,
" Their summits glowing with celestial fire,
" Whilst hope is ne'er beguil'd by vain conceit—
" The heart's arch-enemy.   This mortal foe
" Like Satan in the paradise of man
" Would bid him be a god, yet give him death.
    " Pride and conceit hold large dominion here
" And ever rule with despot sway the plain ;
" Their votaries spurn the plan benificent
" Which, making all things differ, levels all.
" But choosing their own way in discontent
" Proclaim each as the other everywhere.
" That man is equal, from one pattern cast

" Like moulded clay, or forms from molten bronze;

" Nor see that e'en a cast may faulty prove,

" Or that the metal may not well anneal ;

" Reviling rulers, they the rul'd annoy,

" In vain pursuit of self aggrandisement.

" As well proclaim the forest trees alike,

" Their uses one, and uniform their lives ;

" The oak should claim the lithesome willow's part,

" The willow's equal right should plough the main;

" But each to other equal in its sphere

" Will not supply each other's separate use ;

" No more than lead be priz'd as purest gold,

" Or either, fill the needed iron's place—

" So nature classifies yet levels all,

" 'Tis man's conceited heart alone rebels

" And strives to struggle 'gainst the law,

" That but in ratio, sees the truest proof

" Of real equality. No flowers that grow—

" Nay, no two hearts or faces are alike

" Or ever will be, whilst creation lives.

" But who shall question of their equal worth

" In the great scheme that leavens everything.

" A thousand chords are strung and tun'd alike,

" And thus the heart's own harmonics are wrought,

" As each one takes the tone he loves the best,

" And forms from that his diapason true.

" But shall the trumpet-voice contemptuous hold
" The tuneful reed whose notes enthral the soul ;
" Or sweetest flutes, lament their low estate
" That cannot tear the welkin into shreds ?
" Such are the hearts of men, and nature makes
" The whole harmonious by their varying powers.
" And thus alike in all the changeful forms
" Creative nature cloth'd that essence-life,
" Are thoughts and impulses—and all the things
" Thou hast and knowest in a ratio true.
" E'en thou, despite the fairest form of man
" Thou see'st, would'st not with him make inter-
      change.
" Or if permitted to become another,
" Cloth'd with his excellence of every kind
" As far as visible, thou would'st not change
" Thy special world of heart—thy subtle sense
" Of something worth retaining for thyself
" With him all unconditional, and be
" No more thine own, but his embodiment.
" If with thy counterpart, thou would'st not change
" (In all things thy superior as thou deem'st)
" How can it be encompass'd in the mind
" That thou would'st barter bodies with the boor.
    " Thou knowest not the life that is around
" Above—below—interior and occult ;

" Thou see'st as in a mirror, but thyself,
" Again repeated, and to that one law
" Thou chainest down the fabric of the brain
" That dares the argument. But did thy mind
" E'er lose its pride of self supremacy,
" And think upon thy fellow of the zones,
" Torrid or frigid, pigmy form or huge,
" Soul and body in creation equal ;
" But yet whose wants, whose pleasures, nay whose
 tones
" Thou canst not understand or fathom ?
" Still more than that, and to a lower depth
" (As thou would'st say) the things not of thy kind,
" Birds—from the martial eagle to the wren ;
" Or beasts, of forest wilds the primal lords,
" Down to that puny pilferer, the mouse ;
" Fish—from Leviathan that beats the waves
" Into a tempest-chorus with his tail,
" Down to the minnow, dancing in the stream ;
" From gayest insect tinsell'd by the sun,
" Or travelling the interminable grass,—
" Down to the life, that swarms to spirit eyes,
" In forms prolific on a grain of sand.
" Thence to the elements whose gaseous forms
" Instinct with life seem but of spirit realms
" Sent to earth's breathing things that they may live.

" With none of these wouldst thou make interchange
" Conceiving (rightly for thy state) thyself the chief.
" But dost thou think that there exists a thing
" In fair creation's ever varying forms,
" That coming from the dust, as e'en thyself,
" And living, as thou liv'st, by favor high,
" Deems his condition worthless, or imperfect,
" That does not hold his own economy
" The subtlest good ?   Nay, if his thoughts could speak
" And reach thy comprehension at a bound,
" Would spurn, with shuddering gesture, change with thee.
   " And sometimes when the heart in its surmise
" Would paint an angel,—lost what shape to fix
" Man still retains his own, but envying, clothes
" His ideal self with wings to ride the air,
" Nor sees, the birds and insects he disdains,
" Possess of right, his coveted estate,
" And with triumphant speed, despite his art,
" They pass him by—a laggard in the race.
   " Couldst thou behold the world of life that dwells
" In Neptune's realms, unknown and beautiful,
" Thou wouldst not deem that in thy atmosphere
" Alone is visible the globe itself.
" Forth from their mossy haunts and coral caves,

" Come forth the armèd warriors of the deep,
" To battle with the foe whose shadow shows
" His hostile form athwart their silent camp.
" Passing, repassing, like the sombre clouds
" That flit across a sunny landscape fair.
" Sometimes when Neptune rouses from his couch
" And shakes the rock-bound fastness of his bed,
" Blows with an awful breath his trumpet blast
" To raise the billows from their slumbers soft,
" And wake a tempest worthy of his power,
" Lo! through the upper space descending crash
" The heavy cargoes proffer'd to the storm ;
" A vain surrender!—feeble effort made
" To baffle with a lighter hull the waves,
" And woo the winds to waft it far away.
" A stronger gale!—the heaving billows rise
" And split the struggling vessel in the midst;
" Then Neptune's element awhile is fill'd
" With prizes yielded. Men and treasures too
" Come hurtling through the azure of the sea,
" And Neptune's warriors hail the victory won,
" As Triton sounds the recall of the hosts.
    " So, when in arctic seas, Leviathan,
" O'erthrown by subtle wounds from flying darts,
" Dragg'd from the crimson seas yields up the fight—
" Then baffled Neptune mourns a battle lost.

" Oft too, the warrior sword-fish seeks the foe
" And with his weapon stealthily uprear'd
" Plung'd to its length—withdrawn —and plung'd
 again
" The unsuspected leak secures the prey.
 " And when thou stridest o'er the summer fields,
" Instinct with life as wond'rous as unseen,
" Thy heedless foot hath crush'd a thousand lives
" Into the dust of death at every step,
" How great thou art! how wond'rous is thy power!
" But yet thou know'st it not—for now anon
" Comes on thy kind a whirlwind influence,
" And stricken down in fever, myriads die.
" Thou callest this a plague, a pestilence ;
" It is an unseen spirit passing near,
" Whose mighty wings have stirr'd the air amain,
" Or whose portentous form hath check'd the beam
" That gives the life-tone to the morning air.
" No more the insect slain beneath thy feet
" Can see thy prowess, or thy awful form
" Than thou canst see within thy mortal ken
" The angel-wanderer from world to world.
 " 'Tis well indeed thou see'st with order'd power
" Proportion'd objects—natural or rare.
" All measurement or weight is but the sum
" That to the creatures influenc'd appears

" Approximately needful. What if thou
" Hadst different vision and could see the motes
" In forms terrific, or the host of stars,
" As flaming worlds, roll through the awful space.
" Or, if contracted to a narrower sphere,
" The sun in smaller radiance met thy view,
" Yielding a lesser day?—if midnight hours
" Gave to thine eyes the melancholy moon
" Gilding the vault of night in starless skies,—
" Thy sight, (effacing forms familiar now)
" Could'st only see, like motes the birds of air—
" Thou would'st not be the creature that thou art
" But yet well worthy of the life thine own.
   " Thine art hath prob'd beyond thy nature's ken—
" Thou see'st at will by mediums thou hast made
" The forms else hidden from apportion'd sense ;
" But what avails thy poring gaze beyond
" The cloudy skies that bound thy earthly home,
" Save but to show thine heart how great the power
" That rules and guides the glorious worlds thou
    see'st.
" Not to elate it with a pride that deems
" Itself the thing that is the excellence
" For which creation hath its end alone.
" Or gazing lower—to the things minute,
" Thy works, however fine the mechanism,

" Grow rough and jagged 'neath the microscope.

" But His, in full perfection, hold alike

" The sun itself, or insect of an hour;

" Clothes to thine aided sight with burnish'd gold

" The things that thou would'st follow with thy gaze

" To depths imagination fathoms not,

" In proof triumphant what thou art at best.

   " Oft, when thy tending hand hath rear'd a flower,

" Or fostering care hath shelter'd from the storm,

" Unknown thy kindly art hath sav'd a life,

" Or spar'd the sufferings of a little bird,

" Thou hast fulfill'd a part of nature's law,

" Nor known the deed, nor its effect approv'd.

" So when deep sorrow comes upon thy house,

" And dark despair enwraps thy lov'd and thee,

" Thou only know'st when health and life return

" That all is peace and sunny hope again.

" The angel being that thou canst not see

" Hath borne the healing balm from many a world—

" Hath cull'd the flowers from spheres of spirit life

" And shed their odours on the tainted air.

" Vanquish'd by health from orbs beyond the sun,

" The sorrow-sickness quits thy homestead's verge,

" And onward passing like a beam of light

" The holy messengers unseen attest

" Their varying duties to the God supreme.

" Or when the angel, thus with mission true,
" Folds her bright wing, and claims a sister soul,
" Unseen she enters, and with action brief,
" Strips off the form of clay—life's counterpart:
" Then soul and body strive, and separate.
" Expectant angels for an instant see
" Three forms engag'd in preparation there,
" Of whom but two may join the waiting throng.
" One moment, and the body seems to cling
" Towards the spirit struggling in its grasp—
" 'Tis but an instant—and the earth reclaims
" The wonderous casket that she furnished.
  " Enough! we linger,—but let thy beating heart
" Direct thy gaze.   Behold the bowers of love!
" Thou see'st them close to friendship's pure domain,
" And blending with the outskirts of his realm;
" There seems an ample margin to the bowers—
" But seeming only.   'Tis a hollow ground
" Where many walk, but find the pathway there
" Is scarce enough for two who fairly step,
" Like those of Syracuse, whose virtues won
" Stern Dionysius' pardon and his love,
" E'en on the gloomy scaffold's fated brink.
" But quagmires, treacherous pitfalls, and the like
" Make up the specious realm that friendship claims.
" Yet from his dawning skies love's bowers receive

" Full oft their morn-beams and the air is sweet.

" Already hark the chime! for all around

" This fairy land of love is full of song

" Which thou may'st hear anon when I depart.

" Songs to a mortal's eyes—to Luna's beam—

" To tears, to smiles, to falsehood and to truth.

" E'en birds assist : The lark at earliest morn

" Doth never raise his carol upon high

" To greet the sun, but love-rapt votaries sing

" And imitate the joy that swells his heart.

" The cooing doves provoke soft influence round ;

" Whilst sighing breezes yield a sweet response ;

" And Philomel can see from many a bough

" The listening mortals spellbound with her song.

" Lutes, tun'd to dulcet strains in rosy bowers,

" Echo the love-notes of the vocal grove,

" Whilst jealousy in shades of deep distrust,

" To restless vigils gives the lagging hours.

" Now look once more—the plain extends its range,

" Here lands spread out, here seasons come and go,

" The heart is given to joy, when vernal spring

" Unlocks the streams, and budding blessings show.

" Next high-soul'd courage claims a kingdom fair,

" And rears his banner to the sun-bright heaven—

" When straight appears the summer of the heart.

" See vine crown'd hills in purple clusters glow,

" And jocund mirth is dancing in the vale.

" 'Tis the heart's autumn, and a vast expanse

" Owns its ripe influence. E'en the lands beyond,

" Where winter reigns, receive its genial breath

" To soften there the rigour of its storms ;

" Thus kindly temper'd its calm subjects feel

" No winter in the heart that brings alarm ;

" Though oft the terrors of the changeful sky

" Drive to the utmost verge the pilgrim's steps.

" Thence all is dark—the last and final bound

" Is gaunt despair's black overhanging rock.

" Above, the angry skies portentous frown ;

" Below, are caves all darksome and profound.

" No songs are here—not e'en the curlew's scream

" Breaks on the muttering of the gloomy wind.

" Sometimes a wail ascends from lingering hope,

" (For hope alone is life) no echoed sounds

" Console the broken heart, and silence reigns.

" Despair is not content, though all unmov'd

" The suffering spirit bears a galling chain.

" My mission ends—I cannot show thee all,—

" And thou may'st listen to the varied songs

" That rise upon the ear and tell their tales

" Of selfishness—or trusting faithful love.

" But ere I leave thee to thy chosen path,

" Lift up thine eyes, behold the sun again ;

" Thou see'st it dimly mark'd,—it shines afar,

" But veil'd, and misty through the atmosphere.

" For now athwart the sun see shadowy forms

" By adverse winds and vapours made ; the beams

" Now hidden,—now anon in glory shine—

" So doth the soul obscur'd and dark appear

" When doubts and cavils fill the nether air,

" The heart's religion.   'Tis in vain despair

" Looks for the light of truth to guide the feet.

" No broken heart can heal, save when the air—

" Is pure and gentle with religion's power.

" It casts away the poison from its wounds,

" When rosy atmospheres from spirit bowers

" Bring balms to pacify the aching thing,

" Whose clos`ed wounds shall scarce retain a scar.

" But oft the air is thick with stormy strife,

" Where peace should dwell and love be paramount.

" The suffering heart no healing solace knows

" When storms prevail within religion's realm ;

" When ministers of strife, in guise of peace,

" With thunder-voices shake the pliant air—

" Breathing no hope nor refuge but themselves.

" In fitful gleams the soul shines on the heart,

" Watches the passing of the stormy hour

" That veils in tears religion's atmosphere.

  " Pilgrim, arise !—forth on thy mission speed,

" Thine eyes are opened—be thine ears attun'd—
" For spirit senses, given thee for awhile,
" Will show how hearing may be far improved ;
" How mortal faculties, howe'er acute,
" Fail when they grasp occulted mysteries.
" As gazing on the rolling orbs of space
" Suns beyond suns, and systems bas'd on each,
" The awe-struck mortal with his heart amaz'd
" Abandons sound, and clothes in silence all—
" Takes refuge in the thought that all this joy,
" This rapid intercourse of starry worlds
" Voiceless proceeds, in repetition dumb.
" But when thine ears have caught celestial tones,
" And heard the music everlasting, pour'd
" From earth, from sea, and from resounding spheres,
" Thou'lt note th' harmonious whole, thou'lt well
        detect
" The subtle melody that underlies
" The seeming discord of created things,
" And know that silence hath no space in truth.
" That when the forest leaves unmov'd remain,
" Nor not an echo stirs the placid air
" 'Tis but the mortal sense hath limit reach'd,
" Conceiving nought to be but what it knows.
" The neighbour trees stand jocund in the sun,
" When summer solstices invite to joy ;

" And in the varying seasons well perform
" Each to the other every forest rite.
" To spirit-ears they join the glad refrain
" That breaks from nature in perpetual tones,
" And in the mighty chorus of the wind
" Wrestle in mirth to show their roystering strength;
" Or twine their branches in a tender grasp
" To mourn a comrade stricken down by time.
    " Enough! to thee is given a little while
" To hear the mystic voices of the heart;
" And hark! already on the breeze I hear
" Those coming sounds, that now approaching, tell
" That to the verge of thy desired land
" Thou hast arriv'd.   I leave thee to thyself :
" As for mine ears the sounds have no avail ;
" Yet for thy guidance thou shalt hear from me
" What now I list, and when thy sense attun'd
" Corroborates, thou wilt not soon forget.
" The vocal sounds I note—they come to thee ;
" But thus I now anticipate their words,
" That thou may'st, when repeated, know them well,
" Whether sole melodies or chords divine.
    " Farewell,—no more thou'lt hear my friendly
        voice
" In stern rebuke, or guidance on thy path.
" Listen, they come! remember thou the words

" Again may be repeated on thy way,
" They sing to thee from out those realms afar—
" The heart's domains, — and this their wonted
    song—

" Pilgrim mortal ! curious seeker
" For the things that hidden lie ;
" Though we strive not 'gainst the weaker,
" Each of us in turn a speaker,
" Come to give thy heart reply.

" Seek thy treasure—laugh at sorrow,
" Man of life's bright summer day ;
" There doth come a sure to-morrow,
" That will neither beg nor borrow,
" But will melt thy gold away.

" Seek thy triumph ! child of morning,
" To thy charms, love's votaries bend ;
" Though thou yield but bitter scorning,
" Fatal hands speed thy adorning,
" To recall the gifts they lend.

" Seek thy pleasure !—cold deceiver,
" Broken hearts are at thy feet ;
" Thou shalt yet prove a believer ;
" For there comes a great achiever,
    Who will brook not thy deceit.

" Seek thy laurels—man of glory !
" Victor thou in many a field ;
" Trophies golden—trophies gory,
" Thine they are, and thine the story—
" ' Life is vain,' for thou must yield.

" Seek thy chaplet—poet dreaming !
" Breathe of love, or fame, or hate ;
" Sorrow thine—or rapture beaming,
" All thy truth, and all thy seeming,
" Shall be dark and desolate.

" Seek thy burthen—sorrowing brother !
" Though the world be drear and lone ;
" Thou may'st upward seek another,
" But the earth—she is thy mother,
" And shall claim thee as her own "

END OF FIRST PART

THE
HEART'S CHRONICLE.

PART SECOND.

ARGUMENT.

The Spirits of the Heart having departed after the choral admonition in the preceding chapter—a dreamy feeling arises upon the explorer of the unknown regions, and the second book opens with his apostrophe to sleep and dreams, and leads on to his imaginary introduction to the lands belonging to Faith and Hope, who reproach him in respect to neglected hours of life. He sees the rude or primary state of the heart is contention or state of war, and a description is given in accordance. The book goes on with some of the remainder of the passions and sentiments of the heart, closing with a visit to the abode of Friendship. Sojourn therein and distant prospect of the Lands of Love.

THE HEART'S CHRONICLE.

'Tis sleep, the fount of health, when day is done,
That fills life's brook when parch'd by many a sun.
O plan benificent! with wonders rife!
Foretaste of death! thou art the spring of life.
A thousand forms thy healing arts assume
And airs ambrosial all thy dreams perfume.
No time,—no place, is proof against thy power,
Nor only thine the silent midnight hour;
Nor warmest bed—nor cozy ample chair
Alone thy privilege delightful bear.
Rock'd by the winds beneath the stormy sky,
The sea-boy hears his childhood's lullaby.
The wearied hind upon the hillock flings
His massive frame and seeks refreshing springs.

Awhile he breathes through grassy mediums there
The floral essence of immortal air.
Alike thy kindly spirit weaves a spell
For infant eyelids where thou lov'st to dwell.
The starveling child, flung on a wretched bed,
Sleeps soundly, freed from cruelty and dread.
Delusive dreams sweet childhood's solace yield,
'Midst playmates,—butter-cupp'd—in golden field.
The drunken helot in his miry trance,
Whose brain yet reels in Bacchanalian dance,
In dreams, where many a fount its coolness pours,
Sleeping, the havoc of his frame restores.
Or when the lamp, the curtain'd window shows,
Fainter and paler in the day-beam grows;
The faithful watchers through the fever'd night
Hail with fond hope the dawning of the light,
As they behold the dear eyes closed by thee;
Faith soars to heaven—hope bends in prayer the knee,
That rest from thee a blessing shall impart,
And move to joy the weeping watcher's heart.
But yet, methinks, it is an awful thing
When sleep profound doth death's own image bring,
That when the body to refreshing hours
Hath yielded up its cognizance and powers—
Nor dream, nor fancy hath awak'd the brain,—
But death itself usurp'd a mimic reign;

Where is the spirit in those hours?—yon bell,
Whose tones gave forth their requiem and their knell
Records a truthful warning they have fled
Unknown to sleepers—thus so like the dead.

Hence thoughts bewildering! what delicious air
Awakes desire its balmy source to share?
How brightly clear cerulean morning skies
Invite the footsteps to escort the eyes,
To roam afar to meet the breeze of morn,
And list to every tone from matins borne;
To mark the dewy blessing that e'en yet
Baptising nature grants with fingers wet—
To sanctify, with holiest touch, the hearts
That learn with joy the lessons she imparts.

Forth let me wander in this wonderous land,
Unknown its landscapes, on its sward I stand;
The very turf is thick with thymy flowers,
Which form for unseen things perennial bowers.
Two fluttering birds, behold, are nestling here
Close to the ground, and sharing duties dear;
Sweet pleasures prompt their genial natures too—
These are the lands of faith and hope I view.
The balmy plants I see, with mingled lot
Rise to prolific life in every spot.
I tread them down—they rise again and smile,
And lead me on with many a witching wile.

I pluck them forth—some leaves respond with pain,
But firmly fix'd their rigid roots remain.
" We are the food of hope "—their voices say,
" Poor mortal ! we are springing from thy clay—
" 'Tis thine to bear thy sorrows as decreed,
" But hope must live through every time of need.
" We form her bed when downcast she returns
" From the soul's errand, and for rest she yearns.
" Her mother faith, dwells with her for awhile
" Till storms are past and hearts with pleasure
        smile.
" She tends our weaklings—but receives her food
" From other climes—by us not understood,
" Save that we feel a moistening influence fall
" That stands in gems—in dewdrops on us all,—
" This is faith's task to gather o'er the plain,
" And yield, in grateful tears, to heaven again.
" So press not on our fragile forms severe,
" Lest faith should weep with hope the bitter tear.
" Thou can'st not pluck us from the land we hold,
" Nor buy us with thy stores of mortal gold.
" We are the hours,—small as thou deem'st our
        kind,
" Smaller and less are varied forms behind.
" We grow apace, and, ere thy gaze is done,
" We feel the progress of the rising sun.

" Our kindred gone—the hours thou hast forgot,
" Because our lives too oft, are valued not,
" But left to waste, till,—wonder and amaze !
" We leave hope's homestead for the land of days—
" Where grow the years to trees, whose branches bear
" The fruits of faith and hope, or dark despair."
 Cease to upbraid ! ye mentors of my way,
I toil amidst you in my little day,
I mourn full well the lost ones of your kind,
And seek the faith and hope I yet may find.
Sad as I wander, yet my eyes behold
These happier realms their mysteries unfold.
Lo ! hope ascends on wing of lark upborne,
The welkin echoes with her song of morn,
She leaves her nest on earth, but, lest despair
Usurp at once the objects of her care,
Faith keeps below, and spreads her spirit-wing
Upwards to hope, and prompts her heart to sing.
 O spirit ! now thy gift I well can feel,
No earth-bound sense could bid the tongue reveal
The burning words of that enraptur'd strain
Which moves the heart to joy and peace again.
In these blest regions faith and hope supreme
Give tongues to trees and words to every dream.
Instinct with speech the streams and flowers declare
The transports felt—the raptures that they share ;

Till the full heart, beneath the influence bright,
Derides despair and revels in delight.
So, spirit of the heart I take my way
Through mazy paths that quit the light of day;
Led on by thee to trace the wonted scene,
May faith and hope for ever intervene
To smooth the way and point the better road
That leads me back, when lost, to their abode—
Secure from harmful doubt, where'er I roam,
May their blest realms receive me welcome home.

    Sweet voices! hark! it is an old refrain,
Dear memoried accents charm mine ears again,
Like echoed music is each voice that sings—
I strive to catch the message that it brings,—
Borne on the air and travelling to the heart,
The lingering tones of choral words impart
A guiding influence as I take my way
In search of wonders which these realms display.

    How fair the sunshine on the landscape gleams,
How fair the hills, the woods, and silver streams—
Methinks I sail upon a golden sea,
And then anon I walk with footsteps free—
I fly to dizzy mountain-tops in air,
And then descend to caverns of despair.
One moment yields a foretaste of delight,
Another shows the clouds of coming night.

Is this the kingdom of the human heart
I fain would visit in its every part ?
Is this the realm where tyrant passions reign
O'er vassal chiefs of pleasure and of pain,
Where wild emotion holds her fluttering court
And mad sensation's votaries resort ?
A brilliant sun that lights a summer sky,
Though good and evil undistinguish'd lie ;
A silver moon that brightens every vale,—
Now gentle breezes—now a fearful gale ;—
'Tis the first step I take upon the soil,
I hurry onward, eager for the toil,—
Impell'd the varying attributes to know
And whence the actions and the passions flow.
    The sky hath chang'd,—clouds travel o'er the sun,
Forms of unrest each other over-run ;
Loud voices mingle in confuséd tone,
That each one claims and seems content to own ;
A jargon chorus—discord all complete,
In praises hail their monarch—self-conceit.
These are his lands—extending far and wide,
And bounded by the mountain home of pride.
What swelling tumult fills the air around,
None deign to listen—each gives forth his sound,
And strives by gesture, or by solemn tone
To prove all mortal errors—save his own.

Or raving wildly of the faults he sees,
Awards his rival all iniquities.
Heedless alike of what is lost or won—
Who differs must be knave or simpleton.
Here all are teachers—loudest is the best—
A lull in tumult is ignoble rest.
Surveying nature from the heights of pride,
They see not nature's works on every side ;
For them alone the universe was spread,
They just agree they form its proper head ;
For why should suns and stars shed rays divine
On common things that know not why they shine ?
Save that the sky may be a witness fair,
That they alone its special blessings share.
The sea, subservient to their proud behest,
Rolls but in homage, as their deeds attest :—
All life, all action, bas'd upon the plan
That nothing wond'rous ever lived but man.

But see, Arachne spreads her silken snare
To catch the flying dainties of the air ;
And man, the fisher of the seas and streams,
To nature true, pursues not ideal dreams—
But imitates as best he can her arts,
Right glad to learn the myst'ry she imparts.
Like hers, his toils on other laws but wait
The work of power unseen—the common fate.

He sees the ants in busy traffic share
The seeming burthens of commercial care ;
And lo ! instinctive genius in his heart
Founds an exchange, and institutes a mart.
 Here beauty plays her genial part full well,
And weaves around the heart a holy spell ;
Combin'd with truthful love she gilds the sphere,
And man would seem content that heaven were here.
But beauty hath her mission from above—
For what were all in nature but for love.
Here too conceit his tinsell'd court doth hold,
Here glaring brass declares itself pure gold,
Reviles the histories of the ages gone,
And prates of " progress "—known to him alone.
Old things are bad—for "Progress," wond'rous child !
Cancels the records in Time's storehouse piled,
And deems the sages of the days gone by
Were nature's blanks—created but to die ;
That nothing was of pleasure or of art,
Till pride, call'd progress, rul'd the human heart.
Nor sees that nature—cheated of her name,
Alone performs the deeds conceit doth claim ;
Fails to observe, as blinded by his pride,
Increasing myriads find their wants supplied
By grace, that prompts the heart to seek and find
Occulted stores for needs of every kind.

More men—more wants—more virtue and more vice,
The ratio yet preserv'd—proportion'd nice ;
Thus those who wanted less in days of yore
Had all the joys of moderns wanting more.
How great the mighty ruler of the heart !
Who thus from time to time doth light impart,
That keeps the creatures of the sunny spheres
With knowledge equal to increase and years,—
That all the future—all the past can say
Proves strength is given proportion'd to the day.
　No more I linger, for impell'd I move—
Another region and its scenes to prove.
A throbbing sound that swells into a hum,
Proclaims the approaching plaudits of the drum ;
Now on a primal ground amaz'd I stand
And catch a warlike tone that shakes the land.
Here is the region whence come martial forms—
Here angry winds prevail that sport in storms ;
It is the war-fiend's home—his revel nigh—
He sounds his clarion echoing to the sky ;
A bloody banquet spreads before mine eyes,
And spectre guests and horrid forms arise ;
Wild music fills the regions of the air—
Triumph ! I hear thy song—thy wail, despair !
As numbers thicken by the sounds increas'd,
War's liveried lacqueys hover round the feast.

And when the revel and the rout are done,
And in the west as sinks the crimson sun,
Despite the clang of triumph's martial tones,
Upon the breeze—in fitful gusty moans—
Distracted echo, wandering, doth convey
The sighs and sobs of dear ones far away.
　How strangely blended here are grief and joy—
Death dances nimbly—ghosts with mortals toy.
Yet not obedient to some tyrant lord,
The warrior draws his wild defiant sword ;
Not now for conquest arms the martial host,
Nor creed, nor faith, the once crusader's boast
But science and the progress of the mind,
To arts and virtue not alone confin'd,
Revert to nature in its own wild will,
And culture teaches reason how to kill.
Not the poor triumphs of the ancient days
When merely martial prowess claim'd the bays ;
Or thousands slain by slow and cumbrous power,
Or swift-winged arrows falling as a shower ;
To learning and to genius these must yield,
As slaughter, scientific, sweeps the field.
Now carnage claims from reason all its dues,
Th' unerring shot—the murd'rous mittrailleuse.
Still, as of old, the soldier hails the day,
The morning drum, the evening revel gay.

And Bacchus aids, from regions not afar,
Shedding a sunny gleam upon the war ;
The heart's carouse and glory here combin'd—
A song is borne upon the morning wind.—

" Hark ! hark ! the reveille ! gallant comrades arise,
" Night's vassals retire, there's a streak in the skies,
" And the heralds of morning in splendour are come,
" Hark ! hark ! the reveille ! 'tis the beat of the drum.

" Hence dreams of the darkness—awake then and up,
" Fling troubles away with the dregs of the cup,
" For all there is glory—bright fortune for some,
" Hark ! hark ! the reveille ! 'tis the beat of the drum.

" If to die be our fate—we will die in our might,
" If to live—we will pledge in the wine cup to-night,
" So rouse, comrades rouse, and all dreams overcome,
" Hark ! hark ! the reveille ! 'tis the beat of the drum.

Poor human heart !—are these thy noblest charms ;
Death and despair—the guerdon of thy arms ?
So, in primeval glooms the welkin rings
With yells of savage beasts—the forest kings,
Whose angry passions rival e'en thine own,
Save nature's instincts prompt but theirs alone.
Thou would'st not own their hunger or their hate—
Thy warrior-children hold a nobler state,

With reason blest, they slay without a cause,
And lawless deeds exact,—enforcing laws.
   Sweet spirit lead me on ;—afar I hear
Bright choral strains,—and grateful accents near ;
It is the harvest prompts the genial fire,
The landscape warms and clouds and mists retire.
I hurry onward, lo ! the sunny skies
Have bidden all earth's hidden treasures rise ;
What joy is heard—what songs the welkin fill
From teeming homesteads—from the vine-clad hill ;
The grateful heart now throbs to genial strains
And joy, sunlighted, revels on the plains.
It is the harvest ! and the jocund song
Fills evening haunts, and steals the vale along.
It is the vintage ! and to music sweet
Glance loving eyes, and twinkle dancing feet.
Now Bacchus reigns—the rosy god of wine,
Berries and grapes—the ivy and the vine—
Teem in the glowing autumn of the heart,
Whilst all Apollo's priests their songs impart
In praise of Bacchus,—he whose power can move
The weak to life—the wise to tender love ;—
He whom the crew rebellious, bore away
From Naxos, where a sleeping boy he lay—
As angry waking, prisoner on the sea,
The boy-god used his powers for liberty.

Amaz'n the crew beheld the circling vine
O'er all the ship its clinging arms entwine.
Amaz'd to madness when they saw on board
The stealthy tigers as they roam'd and roar'd ;
No more the Lydian pilot they defied,
But madly plung'd into the foaming tide.
The ship from Naxos held its prow no more,
But, steer'd by friendly hands, regained the shore.
Hail ! kingly friend—O reveller of the sky,
Fill every cup and gladden every eye.
Round every form thy genial mantle throw,
And bid the heart with sunny pleasures glow.
Light ! glorious light ! it is the god appears,
'Tis Bacchus comes, the conqueror of fears ;
The crowding worshippers in every part
Fill all the swelling landscapes of the heart.
    Ye priests of Bacchus ! raise the choral strain,
See conquer'd sorrow vanish from the plain ;
The fount of wine is sparkling in the sun,
The god doth revel in the vintage won.
Sing, mortal sing, and join the choir divine,
'Tis Bacchus lifts the cup, to bless the wine.
" Hail monarch ! " rings upon the vocal gale,
And echoed harmonies respond " Hail ! Hail ! "
What varied light in every stream is seen
The bursting grape, in purple and in green,

Invites to dip in ruby floods or share
The amber brook, or foaming torrent there.
I hear a strain from ivy-crownèd bower,
Where Bacchus hath bestow'd his genial power;
Inspir'd by wine the grateful heart declares,
The varied forms of beauty that it shares;
The sparkling tint—the cascades of champagne—
Sherries—which yet, the sunbeams caught retain.
With purple port his grateful song divide
And float his spirit on a golden tide.
Sing on!—contagious joys to thee belong,
I catch thy strain—and imitate thy song;—

" Glowing, sparkling, bubbling treasure,
" Whence art thou—oh! where thy birth?
" Life is dancing to thy measure,
" Care—carousing blithe with pleasure,
" Laughing claims his comrade mirth;
" Earth doth know thee, thou must reign,
" Bubbling, sparkling, king champagne!
" Let me hail thee, monarch mine—
" Ever, and for ever—wine!

" Changeful, charming, monarch merry,
" In thy robe of sunny guise,
" Crown'd with autumn's ripest berry—
" Yield thy store of amber sherry!

" So shall sunbeams fill our eyes.
" We adore thee—thou may'st be
" Changeful,—charming majesty—
" But I hail thee—monarch mine
" Ever, and for ever—wine!

" Magic ruby! fountain streaming!
" Port! thou rul'st our revelry—
" Glorious vintage, purple beaming—
" We will worship in our dreaming—
" And adore thy source and thee.
" Amber! ruby! sparkling joy!
" Nought shall loyalty destroy,
" Let me hail thee, monarch mine—
" Ever, and for ever—wine! "

Enraptur'd votary! as I grasp thy hand,
I dare not linger in this teeming land;
Lead me aright for thou can'st show the way
To friendship's haunts, nor need I fear to stray;
As led by thee when Bacchus warms the heart,
Hate hides his head, deceit and doubt depart.
Inspir'd, I seem thy mystic joys to share,
And ride with thee upon the buoyant air,—
Evolv'd from friendship's incense-breathing shrine
To raise poor mortals to the realms divine;

Adjoining bowers of roses lend their aid
And sweetest scents from love's own myrtle shade.
   Now quit me Bacchus ! let me seek repose
On this sweet bank which in the sunset glows ;
'Tis friendship's genial homestead that I see:
These truthful ferns awhile my couch shall be.
In this retreat before I enter there,
O let me breathe anticipated air,
And hear the music borne upon its wings
From ærial harps,—from quivering golden strings,
Attun'd by friendship's hand in friendship's hall,
With shining casements in the ivied wall,
And ere I join the group assembled there,
I gaze around and trace the prospect fair.
In this expanse now spread before mine eyes
What crowded ways the outer space supplies,
What mazy walks in circles spread the plain,
And narrower grow for votaries that remain.
Crowded the paths with friendly groups appear,
Each circle leading to a smaller sphere,
Still round they go,—and varying with the sky
The friends of sunshine from the storm-cloud fly ;
For as the space grows smaller in its round,
And narrow pathways lead through slippery
   ground—

They seem to melt away like mists of morn,
Nor dare a path beset with many a thorn,
Shar'd but by few whose undissolv'd regard
Is seal'd by faith, and crown'd by rich reward.

In many a dwelling which my fancy sees,
Falsehood, the mimic, thrives in wealth and ease,
And with a voice of gladness seems to blend
Mysterious accents of dissembling friend;
Till changeful fortune tries the mimic tone,
And wrecks the hearts of faithless ones alone;
Then crowds disperse—the motes of sunny rays,
And lonely pathways tell of cloudy days.
In vain the false ones hail each passing guest,
They know no more the halcyon home of rest;
Until at last—from every hope exempt,
They crave the mute, mild mercy of contempt.
O 'tis no light thing that we have a friend
Whose heart is pure, whose virtues never end.

Yet see! through devious ways and darken'd hours
Hearts that are true in sunbeams and in showers,
Still knit together in a holy bond,
Ne'er heed the troubled way but look beyond.
Till left together in the purer space
The way to friendship's inner bower they trace,—
A little temple, shining like a star,
Rewards the toiling pilgrims from afar,

Where dwells content—where angry passions cease,
And pleasure is the servitor of peace.
Life's pulses throb with hallow'd memories dear,
Uncheck'd by falsehood —unassail'd by fear.
I cannot rest—but to the goal I move—
Friendship! I come thy attributes to prove,
Thy portal opens to my signal now,
I am the welcome guest, the master—thou.
All fears, all idle fancies now depart
Thy welcome gives a life-throb to the heart.
  O friendship! what a vast domain is thine,
What varying sorrows and what joys combine,
What solace doth thy blessed power impart,
And yield, of heaven a foretaste in the heart.
At once I sit as bidden to thy board,
And share the joys thy votaries afford ;
A voice of sweetest tone its influence brings,
And thus thy chosen song with gladness sings :—

" What is it gold can never buy,
" To yield the heart its earthly bliss,
" Say is it beauty's tender sigh,
" O tell me lovers, is it this ?
" Then, dreaming poet, is it fame,
" Whose wealth can raise thee to the sky,
" Whose breath shall give a transient name,
" Is this what gold can never buy ?

" O crave not love, for that can be
" A fleeting passion of the mind,
" Nor vainly trembling, bend the knee
" To fickle fortune's passing wind.
" Pure friendship of the heart alone
" Is life's perennial ecstasy,
" Though poor the dwelling it may own,
" It is what gold can never buy."

The song is done, I see the moonlight gleam
Full on the casement with her lovely beam;
I gaze without upon the starry skies,
And far away new scenes enchant mine eyes;
For lo! a little path I seem to trace,
That from the temple leads to outer space.
A garden walk—a flowery border'd way,
Where youths seem waiting for the breaking day.
I fain would follow, yet awhile I seem
Held back by friendship's hand as in a dream.
Yes! friendship bids me linger on my way,
Whilst many a votary tunes his cheerful lay.
Though speed the hours awhile in converse sweet,
As kindred thoughts in interchanges meet;
Here yet inthrall'd my spirit yearns for flight,
And fain would roam those scenes which meet my sight
The open'd casement yields a cooling breeze,
Wafting the murmur of the sighing trees.

A lovely light gilds yonder fairy land ;
On high the queen of night doth all command.
Upon the stilly air love's sighs prevail,
And sobbing music prompts the nightingale,
As from the thorn, in dread of day too soon,
She sings her gushing song and woos the moon.
Entranc'd I gaze—'tis loveland's bowers I see,
Charming the heart to tears of ecstasy ;
A firm, but gentle grasp doth bid me stay
Till morn shall gild with light of truth the way ;
O'erpower'd I yield to promis'd friendship's aid,
To light you path of roses now in shade.
The casement closes, and the curtain'd pane
Brings me to earth and all its toils again.
By joy o'erwhelm'd—with myriad thoughts opprest,
I yield to friendship's mandate, and to rest.

END OF SECOND PART.

THE
HEART'S CHRONICLE.

PART THIRD.

THE HEART'S CHRONICLE.

ARGUMENT.

The night having been passed in the halls of friendship, the Pilgrim goes forth at early morning in quest
of the adjacent Lands of Love.   Description of Loveland
—its varied aspects, and its inhabitants.   On the
confines of Loveland are the realms of Deceit, passing
through which the Pilgrim reaches the abodes of Regret
and Despair.   Overwhelmed in the darkness of despair,
he is rescued by the return of the Spirits who direct him
to the light encircling the sacred volume lying on the
path before him, which is the Heart's Chronicle.—
Conclusion.

THE HEART'S CHRONICLE.

PART THIRD.

The night is charm'd away, the silent train
Fades like the dream that hovers o'er the brain;
Far in the west the queen of night hath mov'd,
And borne her spells from loving and the lov'd;
Her pale wan face gives just a lingering look
To mark her faded image in the brook;
No more her cresset lights the vault afar
But melts away with each belated star;
Night hears no more the song-bird or the tale;
Gone is the moon, and hush'd the nightingale.
The amber morning every thought invites
To holy matins, and to heart-delights;
The sun-bright summits in their worship glow,
And grateful prayers are rising from below;

The birds of morning see from every nest
Sweet flowers arise in opening beauty drest;
The blossom'd thorn, that bore the night bird's tales
In sweet devotion fragrant prayer exhales;
Each dreamer waking from melodious spells
Forgets the story told by fairy belles.
 I see thee Loveland—now thy tones I catch,
And quitting friendship's home, I lift the latch;
At once I hurry on the lighted way
To hail the glimpses of the orient day.
 O glory of the heavens! I love thy beams,
Thou dwell'st on hills—thou art upon the streams,
I know thy light, yet see in mute surprise
Another Helios kindling yonder skies.
Thy steeds ascend the zenith and retire
Adown the western steep in crimson fire;
Thee! bright Aurora wakens to the day,
And mounts thy car, companion of thy way.
The flowers peep forth thy welcome face to see,
And yield their homage to thy friend and thee.
But lo! athwart the fair and ample space
A pure, and bright, unchanging beam I trace;
It shines with ray unfaltering and serene,
Without a night or cloud to intervene;
It claims no star as medium from above,
But straight from heaven descends, the beam of love.

Thou Loveland! brightest empire of the heart,
From thy pure centre varying rays depart,
Which fall on soils all varying in degree,
Claiming thy rights in fair equality.
Some far away just catch thy ray divine,
With mingled light from other stars that shine ;
Thus colder grown, to earthly influence given,
Ne'er yield a perfect love—the gift of heaven.
Already now the outward tones I hear
That tell me bowers of love I venture near ;
Now on the outskirts of the mystic space,
Where love doth sing or beauty move in grace,
The charméd breeze that sweeps the fairy land,
Breathes serenade, or echoes saraband.
The morning sun my onward path hath shown,
The roses bloom around love's portal grown—
I pass the bound, and lo! before my gaze
A hundred paths diverge, and varied ways,
Which, like a labyrinth, the pilgrim vex—
Joy, bath'd in tears, with pleasure doth perplex ;
But e'en the mists which rise from tears of love
Mount the pure air, and meet the rays above—
E'en as of old the covenanted bow
Gleam'd from the cloud that cast its gloom below,
So doth love's rainbow span the hopeful sky,
Inspiring faith—love's immortality,

And sunlit sorrow, and dissolvéd fears
Gleam on the heart—the covenant of tears.
　'Tis early—but the songsters of the bowers
With Flora join'd anticipate the hours,
Whilst tuneful swains, partakers of their joy,
To love their voices raise in rapt employ.
Now bright as morning's self looks forth a maid
From the watch'd lattice, tenderly survey'd
By eyes that early chas'd the night away
To wake with rapture on love's holiday.
It is his song!—I see the happy swain,
Whose accents warble with an old refrain,
I needs must listen, for the song doth bring
Some voicéd dreams again on memory's wing.

SONG.

" Hasten dearest! see the morning!—
　　Dancing sunbeams through the trees
　Seem to chide thy slow adorning,
　　Whilst sweet birds sing symphonies.
　Songsters blithe the sun are greeting,
　　And in nature's wonted way
　The old, old story are repeating,
　　As they make love's holiday.

" Let us cheat the dewy hours,
　　Till the sun is up on high—

Then chaplets weave of morning flowers
'Neath the forest's canopy ;
Whilst the sun in noontide glory
Casts his fierce meridian ray,
Memory brings the old, old story
To beguile love's holiday.

" When sinks the day-god faint and weary
To his crimson couch of rest,
We will on our pathway cheery,
Greet the twilight in the west.
'Neath the moonlight in the valley
We will linger on our way,
With the old, old story dally,
And recall love's holiday."

'Tis early yet, and scarcely have I trod
The sweet parterres that variegate the sod,
Or fairly mark'd the paths that lead away
To wonderous realms that Loveland's laws obey ;
Still music wakes and every vocal grove
Melodious echoes where love's minstrels rove.
Already too I see on either hand
A chequer'd pathway doth divide the land ;
Each hath its entrance from obstructions clear
That none may halt in doubt, or faint with fear.

One portal woos the eye with moss o'ergrown—
The sign by which maternal love is known
And hath inscribed upon its circling wall,
" Who enters here shall ne'er know love's recall."
The other hath a golden lattice bright
And many a flower performs its mystic rite ;
The blue-eyed pimpernel with many a wile
To love's sweet assignation doth beguile,
Roses and myrtles fill up many a space
Whilst lilac lends its love-emotion'd grace ;
A thousand charms, and emblems sweet invite
To win the footsteps to its portal bright,
O'er which inscribed, my wondering fancy reads
" Who flieth conquers—who pursueth bleeds."
    O ! what the love that never knows recall
Nor change, whate'er of sorrow may befall,
But dwells within that love-inspired land
Where peace doth rule with magic hazel wand.
No other home could boast th' inscription there
Or so proclaim the triumphs of its care ;
'Tis love ! maternal love, no coldness knows,
Whose altar fire, once kindled, ever glows,
Whose garden yields but simple things and fair,
Nor envious bramble deals its thorn wound there ;
But garlands sweet with honeysuckle bound
Shed influence dear and odours all around ;

And when affection lists the passing bell
There bloom the amaranth and the asphodel.
Here are no votaries—here no rivals meet,
Calm is the air, and sacred the retreat ;
Passion hath fled the region pure and fair,
And love, for ever watchful, lingers there,
Sings like a seraph to the throne above,
Rapt tearful songs of gratitude and love ;
Shines a calm spirit o'er the troublous wave —
A lonely pole-star, beaming but to save ;
Sits a lorn watcher o'er the stormy strife,
And whispers hope amidst the throes of life.

Parental love ! oh ! who hath not received
The dear devotion, or its spirit grieved ;
Who hath not felt an influence kindly shed,
Which rebel thoughts had deem'd for ever dead.
Through life's long vista who can fail to trace
The memoried sorrows of its angel face ;
But listening oft to cheering sounds that fall
From tuneful breezes that the past recall,
Though time hath bade the wingèd periods fly,
Hears the refrains of childhood's lullaby.

'Tis written, how a king with wisdom blest,
Of yore did mark love's true maternal test ;
When the two mothers clamorous in their woe
Would not the living child of one forego.

Judgment invok'd ! which mother is beguil'd
Whose is the dead, and whose the living child ?
See, when the sword is order'd from its sheath
To render equal both, in mutual death—
" Give her the child " the rightful mother cries,
A voice (she hears alone) the deed denies—
Bids her forego the issue of the strife,
And prove that she who gave, must save the life.
   Lo ! when beneath the sun's meridian blaze,
The little star still shines with hidden rays,
While splendours pour from the ethereal blue,
Still lives the tiny light, unseen, but true ;
Shines when the shadowy hours of evening loom,
And twinkles hopefully amidst the gloom ;
When gone the garish light of transient day,
Night's phantoms seem dispell'd beneath its ray.
So doth maternal love in morning prime
Withold its light amidst the sunlit time ;
The happy heart scarce knows its depth of cares,
Nor e'en suspects the light of love it bears,
Till shadows, borne on sorrow's weary night,
Call forth the loving star's refulgent light—
Upon the heart recipient, then is sent
The holiest beam in nature's firmament.
   I see, yon beckoning boy invites to tread
His winding way of thorns, with flowers o'erspread ;

I follow him impell'd by mystic fate,
And hurry onward through the golden gate,
To tread the enchanting mazes that appear
To close around, bewildering the career—
Perchance they lead when toils and griefs are past
Where both the lands of love unite at last.

Lead on thou vagrant of the rosy hours,
I lose thee sometimes hidden 'midst the flowers;
Where wilt thou lead, in these bewitching bowers?
Say, wilt thou lead me where the voice of truth
Prompts every vow and promise of thy youth,
Where gold hath lost its charm in mortal eyes,
And faith remains of trusting love the prize?
Where braggarts are not—where no syren sings,
And thou thyself art seen without thy wings.
Say, canst thou live the solace of the heart,
Nor always plume thy pinions to depart?
Thou dost not answer, save in dubious smiles,
And on thou speedest with thy wanton wiles.
O'er hill—through valley, leaving hopes and fears,
And lingering fondly by the lake of tears.
For well thou knowest that thou and sorrow share
The springs that flow in many a streamlet there;
Sorrow, thy servant, waits in many a guise
To draw the gushing torrent from the eyes;
Thy rival death doth follow sorrow's train,
But oh! they strive with thee for tears in vain;

Thy victim hath no hope if thou depart,
And hopeless love shall drown in tears the heart.
This then the motto on the golden gate,
That those who will not trifle with their fate,
Who when they catch thee nestling in the heart
Bind fast thy wings, or bid thee to depart;
To use, or lose thy wings the choice alone,
Flying thy wiles, they conquer—thou must own ;
Or spurning all thy tears—thy humble need
A follower makes of thee, but weak indeed ;
They bleed from darts that ne'er yet pity knew
Who bear a wounded heart and thee pursue.

I see thee waiting, for thou lingerest yet,
Nor dar'st the bound where dwells thy foe, regret,
Lest songs which tremble from his shady grove,
Where sigh the votaries of unhappy love—
Should mar the tones thou lovest best, and bring
The discord unrequited love doth sing.
But ere we reach the shades of sad regret—
Deceit's domains, wide spreading, must be met.
Of all the lands the heart doth hold in thrall,
This is the largest, and o'er-rules them all.
His temple everywhere—his castle flings,
As sung of old, its height " above all things."
So safely, thou, sweet love, wilt dare no more
Than thine own bounds to lead me wandering o'er;

Thy moonlight ramblers whisper all around ;
Youth laughs, and echo mimics every sound ;
Methinks sweet bells are ringing everywhere,
'Tis echo, chiming songs upon the air—
Songs from the birds in every vaulted grove
Mingle with tender roundelays of love.
　　I cannot linger for my fate decrees
Onward to move, nor dwell in scenes like these,
Ere I depart, sweet love, O bring again
One minstrel more, and let me hear his strain
Singing to thee,—sweet hope within his breast—
May joy for ever crown his home of rest.
Love, spare thy wounds, O bid deceit depart
With all its wiles, nor wreck the trusting heart.
Listen in pity to a slave of thine
In raptur'd worship at thy purest shrine.
He sings his heart's love—tis a worthy theme,
If love but deign to realize his dream.
She—is his dream of night that fades too soon,
His star of morning, and his flower at noon ;
The fire of love burns bright, when pure the flame,
And this his song, in homage to her name.

Song.

" There is a star I see at morn,
　　When matin prayers to heaven are breath'd ;
　　So softly bright—like hopes new born,
　　When dreams with flowers of love are wreath'd ;

Soon noon-tide glory hides its light,
Then a sweet flower with joy I see;
And twilight ushers in the night,
To bring the star of morn to me.

" O lovely star! O beauteous flower!
What bliss were mine—unchang'd and bright;
Might I but live life's transient hour,
In this sweet spell of dear delight.
Thee in my heart at twilight's gloom—
My dreams of night alone of thee,—
Thou art my fancy's noontide bloom,
Thou art the star of morn to me.

" I ask not why the noontide flower,
A spell of joy doth round me weave—
Why dreams of love at midnight hour
From twilight thoughts a charm receive.
But flower at noon, or dream at night,
Or twilight charm of witchery,
All fade—when in thy love and light,
Sweet star of morn! thou shin'st on me."

Minstrel, farewell! O love! whate'er thou art,
Thou bears't on mortal fate a wond'rous part;
Thine every road is fill'd with travellers gay,
Nor age nor care avoid thy tender sway;

But close upon thy confines,—errant feet
Stray o'er thy bounds, and palter with deceit ;
And then beguil'd the hapless ones declare
Thou art a fiend—a syren of despair.
But lo! they see not they have lost the road
And wander'd, heedless, to deceit's abode—
Where ev'ry blessed virtue of the soul
Hath its sure counterfeit in part or whole ;
Beneath a mask reality to hide,
To cheat the proud heart in its very pride,
Weep with the mourner simulated grief,
And doubting, listen with a feign'd belief.
Yes! I am wandering in the very land—
I go from bowers of love—and trembling stand
On ground that scarcely will my feet sustain,
Whose slipp'ry paths I essay but in vain.
Deceit, I know thee! and can trace thee yet,
Too soon and sorely thou and I have met,
I will not tread thy ways nor hear thee speak,—
Smiles in thine eyes, and tears upon thy cheek ;
Thy hand extended with a welcome fair—
I search thy sleeve and find a dagger there.
    Slave of deceit! thy tyrant lord demands
Thy sleepless eyes and thy untiring hands ;
Thy youth—a fraud upon a guileless heart,
Thy prime—a satire on life's better part,

Thy age, distorted memory makes a grave
For hopes that liv'd,—and, dying—thee forgave;
Yet poor thy triumph small the victory won,
If ought remain unconquer'd, thou'rt undone.
Then go, weak slave, seek thou another foe,
With all thy vaunting, all thy falsehoods—go;
There is one victory yet awaits thy aim,
One triumph more corroborates thy fame;
A dream of memory comes across thy brain,
And thou art young and artless once again.
A name is heard—forgotten long ago,
And murmur'd truths for none but thee to know;
Tears!—such as those by pure affection shed,
When hearts are riv'n in anguish for the dead—
Fall from thy waking eyelids, and declare
Thou hast deceiv'd thyself—O victory rare.
    Deceit! what forms thou dost assume to win
The heart to trust thee in thy greed of sin;
Lo! in thy temple worshipping I see
The votaries self-conceit hath sent to thee,
I pass'd his lands, and saw their busy pride,
And find that he and thou art close allied;
The braggart brawler draws his stores from thee;
Thou mak'st him seem what he assumes to be;
The pious heart too meek thou makest bold,
And self-denial takes contemnéd gold,

So too, beneath thy gentler mimic sway
Hearts die for love, but live yet many a day.

    Tyrant! I pass thy bound, and thee forget,
I travel onward to thy realm,—Regret;
I shake the miry trouble from my feet
That clings to travellers passing through deceit;
Breathing a calmer and a purer air,
That seems a sombre tint on all to bear;
The sun hath veil'd the glory of his beams
And wakeful pilgrims seem entranc'd in dreams.

    Here flow two springs—one bitter and one sweet,
And both gush forth in every cool retreat;
The heart regretful here—in hope secure
Hath sorrow's balm, which sweetly doth endure.
Deceiv'd by death alone with hope not dead,
The object mourn'd, but not the passion fled—
'Tis memory's fond regret prevails alone,
Love sits with hope and emulates her tone;
But whilst regret doth rule with tranquil sway
Mourning the object lov'd and pass'd away,
It drinks sweet waters from the faithful spring
And lives with hope refresh'd—remembering.

    The bitter stream alas! flows far and wide;
Too oft it mingles in life's ebbing tide;
It runs a scorching torrent o'er the heart,
Burning the soil in every fertile part;

Like lava down the steep, it bears away
All flowers of hope that once were bright and gay;
Fell sorrow, led by disappointment, drinks
The bitter draught and in perdition sinks.
  O thou regret! though calm thy votaries move,
Thou hast thy songs to hatred or to love,
Whilst gentle airs from memory's chosen part
Breathe olden joys that echo round the heart.
Too oft from nests in many a lowly spot
Thy fledglings chirp unseen, and heeded not;
Yet all the heart for pain or joy can store,
Dwells in thy treasur'd melodies of yore.
Thou art a tuneful bird 'midst winter's snow;
Thou com'st like spring to bid life's blossoms blow
From every tree that doth a shadow cast,
I hear thy music, birdling of the past!
Thy song alike doth smiles and tears recall
To every spot the heart doth hold in thrall;
Save where deceit doth hold his treacherous land,
Where not a tree to shelter thee will stand,
There dwell'st thou not, nor e'en one fledgling know,
For memory's nest is fill'd with melting snow,
Whose soft white down at first doth tempt thy fate
Then melts to tears and leaves thee desolate.
  O bitter by-gones! how they crowd around!
What angry accents come from hate profound!

When memory on his cold and sunless shore
Recalls dark hours that wreck'd the joys of yore!
The pensive listener on yon bank reclin'd
Doth hear a voice borne on the muttering wind,
Can tell its questioning import which as yet
Seems chiding memory that could so forget.
Still the refrain persistent seems to be,
I hear it too—" dost thou remember me?"
Charging on memory this unwonted strain,
And starting up with unforgotten pain,
He answers echo on resounding air;
And this the strain committed to her care—

" Remember thee? oft doth my heart recall
" The vanish'd hours of joy that once I knew,
" When as I mov'd, like moonlight on a wall—
" A gentle light did cast my shadow true—
" A beam of light, and yet a woman merely,
" I do remember, and, O how sincerely—
" Love worshipp'd her so fondly and so dearly—
" That 'twould be strange if my poor heart forgot,
" Thou art not she, and memory knows thee not.

" Remember thee? Stay, dreaming spirit stay!
" Whilst I recall when launch'd upon the sea,
" And when o'ertaken by a darksome day,
" I saw a welcome signal made to me—

" A beacon light whose guidance sorely needing,
" I took its course—to fatal rocks but leading—
" A demon mock'd me terror-struck and bleeding.
" I do remember thee—I see thee now—
" Thine were the fatal wiles,—the wrecker—thou!

" Remember thee? ah! let long sunless years
" Thine unseen presence bitterly attest;
" Or ask my soul why sad, degrading tears
" Unbidden gush'd from eyelids of unrest.
" Ask if the hermit spirit yet remembers
" The bright fire—cheering all the gone Decembers,
" Whilst lonely gazing on the chilly embers.
" Then still the soul gives back its one reply,
" Not to remember will but be to die."

Yes! memory thou art but an earthly bird;
Oft is thy song by vexéd sorrow heard;
How oft thou spread'st thy wings o'er many a track
From far off nests to bring a fledgling back!
To mourning hearts thou show'st a twinkling star,
And backward roamest o'er the scenes afar;
One treasur'd pledge of joy beneath thy wing,
A by-gone day of hope thou lov'st to bring;
Thou bear'st a blessed spell within thy breast,
Tears are assuaged and weary hearts at rest;
Restor'd are dear ones, lost in infant years,
To mothers now all joyous in their tears;

To hearts estrang'd thou bring'st an olden vow,
Which hope doth hear in repetition now.
Thy mission to the scenes and days that were,
Brings back a tiny lock of yellow hair,
Upon an infant head perchance it grew,
Or dear one still remember'd though untrue.
    Fly, memory, fly! O spread thy wings once more
Bring back sweet hours and parted loves restore ;
Unite the hearts in thy dear treasur'd truth,
By seas divided in their yearning youth ;
Restore the sun-bright scenes of long ago,
And change the aged parent's dream of woe.
Come in thy brightness o'er the boundless main
And bid the widow claim her lov'd again.
Joy in thy song shall baffle winter's gloom,
And in revived spring the heart shall bloom.
And yet methinks these grey and sombre skies
Portend but grief, whilst memory's birdlings rise,
As though the air were thick with wingèd things
That rise disturb'd and flap their startled wings ;
That seem to wait expectant of command,
To travel backward to each o'er past land ;
To seek forgotten pledges and restore
The heart's lost souvenirs of joy once more.
    But lo! the sky gleams forth a blaze of light,
The gloomy griefs have fled like dreams of night ;

Hope and regret are walking hand-in-hand,
And in the glory of their spells I stand.
Yes! hope is pointing to cerulean skies,
And bids regret look up with loving eyes,
Shows him the realm, where in the day to come,
Undying love shall reinstate his home.
O sweet reward for woes in life endur'd
All faults forgiven, all future joys assured,
O memory, thou'rt the minion of regret,
And pain's dark hours thy song doth not forget;
Not only thine the sunshine of the heart,
But in its cloudy scenes thou bear'st a part—
Thy cup so mingled that the draught betrays
The bitter fountain quaff'd in other days;
Thou need'st must drink, — thy song at once
        estrang'd—
And bright no more—the very chord is chang'd;
How sweetly sad thy tone, how sadly sweet!
Yet sing again,—thy mournful tales repeat,—
For now methinks I listen to thy strain—
A sadder theme comes on my ear again;
So changeful thus, why do thy notes recall
The errant passions that the heart enthral?
O hast thou wander'd back—that thou dost burn
With frenziéd thoughts impatient of return;—
Hath heard the tale replete with falsehood's wiles,
And seen again the tears and treacherous smiles;

Hath brought from far off years and vernal shores
The faded trophies memory restores ?
Pale promises like spectres wake again,
And fervent vows renew their lives in vain.
Sing then, sad memory, if thou wilt, a song,
That to these relics of the past belong ;
A wedding favor, or a lock of hair—
The prizéd garment of a faithless fair—
A faded shawl—a ribbon once so gay—
Or golden pledge of long forgotten day.
　　Silent for these—thou sing'st not of thy store,
Go spread thy treasures on the Stygian shore ;
Lost memory's notes should sadden all the air,
And sink the vocal slaves of mute despair.
But lo ! as if thy song should yet be heard,
Though thou art silent, thou most truthful bird,
Faithful thy song though sorrow be thy theme,
Thou bring'st from far across Time's gloomy stream ;
Upon a willow trembling oft I see
The harp of many a string attun'd to thee ;
In changeful impulse like the human mind,
Its cadence wanders on the vagrant wind.
　　Harp of the air ! Æolian spirit hear !
Dream of bright hopes ! and harbinger of fear !
What power divine is brooding o'er thy strings
As every breeze its memoried influence brings !

The listening ear in ecstasy recalls
A voicéd charm that lived in olden halls,
Joins in the revels of the fairy train,
And travels homeward to the lov'd again.
Anon thy torrents foam, and rushing pour
Adown the craggy steep, and shake the shore;
Fear sees the lightning cleave the fancied sky,
And hears the roar that drown'd the seaman's cry;
Again the lull that comes upon thy strains,
Again sweet peace is smiling on the plains;
The heart responsive with its golden chords,
Sets many a tune to sympathetic words,
And joy or sorrow, as thy strains dictate,
Come from thy strings in unison of fate.

Behold! some tender one hath hung in air
His harp, to murmur forth a by-gone care—
Chided by memory's music of the past,
Thus to the winds he doth the sorrow cast;
That hope's regretted love be ne'er forgot,
He hangs the harp on high and stays it not;
I hear the plaintive prelude of the breeze,
And scan the measure of its harmonies;
I see a gentle form in sables clad,
Glide o'er the pathway calm but sweetly sad;
Youth on the brow her coronal hath set,
Moisten'd with dewy tears by kind regret,

Who hath no frowning memories to bring,
But all of hope and every sacred thing.
Sing harp to sorrow! but not hopeless woe,
Tell of her grief that doth in calmness flow,
Peace in her heart and faith within her soul,
She comes with love, that owns not Time's control;
Regret doth hearken in his own retreat—
Sing muse the strain that thou would'st fain repeat,
Which mov'd thee well when on thy sight she came
A youthful mourner with a widow'd name;
The chord is struck which echoes sweet prolong
And thus the muse essays its simple song—

 " Poor child of sorrow—thee I sing,
  But yesterday a nymph of spring,
  Pleas'd was thine ear with cuckoo's voice,
  As far and near, it baffled choice;
  Leaving the mind all doubtingly
  That 'twas no bird for eyes to see;
  But some sweet call from fledgling thing
  To summon forth the fairy spring;
  Whose buds should furnish sweet and fair
  A bridal wreath for thee to wear.

 " I sing of sorrow—but sweet bells
  Chime yet in memory's sunny dells,
  I see thee in thy beauty's hour—
  And in thy hair the bridal flower,

Whose perfume breathes sweet parting sighs
To childhood's home and memories.
Ah ! 'tis a dream of shortest date,
I mark thee now all desolate ;
And by the garb bereav'd ones wear,
Thy homestead hath its vacant chair.

" I sing of sorrow ! who shall guess
The measure of death's bitterness.
I see thy sadness yet how sweet
Thy gaze is cast on friends who greet,
Who fondly hope thy purer mind
Sweet solace from the world may find.
Thou hast thy solace—on thy cheek,
Dear memories crowd and whispering speak
That thou shalt triumph o'er thy woe
Immortal in life's overthrow."

I hear no more the sighing of the strain,
For now a wind sweeps o'er the lyre again,
In vain I strive to catch the fitful tale,
The sounds are wild, and discord doth prevail ;
As lull'd again, the pensive breezes creep,
The tale seems mutter'd to its final sleep.

But hark ! a wail breaks on the troublous air
From songless concaves,—confines of despair ;
Not thine regret ! for in thy truest tones
The heart yet loves the sorrow that it owns ;

But thine despair—fell tyrant of the heart,
Thine, whence the hopeless souvenirs depart.
Say, do I wander to thy sunless shore
Where love and light shall mingle joys no more;
Where deathless vows are riven by the laws
That give to crime the semblance of a cause;
Devotion weeping,—vice without a tear,
Or guilty passion urging its career?
Alike the solace by the law endors'd,
Behold! Despair, thy victims—the divorc'd.
In vain they move in golden fetters bright,
Seen by no eyes whilst shines delusive light,
A galling chain wrapt round the beating heart,
Rankles the wound of memory's fixèd dart,
Which in delirious dreams doth bring again
The days once theirs, in retrospective pain.
No more by moonlight sweetly hand-in-hand,
The lov'd of youth in happier hours they stand;
No more the kiss, so real in dreamy truth,
No more the vows—all justified in youth—
Survive the ordeal of the waking sense,
But melt away in tears of penitence.
Here then to misery comes the sad farewell,
That doth its hopeless tale of sorrow tell;
Here many a Byron mourns—nor yet can pour
His melting verse to live for evermore;

Here many an Ada,—child of happier days!
Dwells in these realms, nor owns a father's lays.
Parted yet visible to mental sight,
She seems to cast o'er passing years a light
That shows alone, her love the dusky way
To shades of peace, beyond life's fever'd day.
Yes! 'tis farewell, O word of deepest power,
Which time doth bring in late or earliest hour.
　Child of the erring! what a spell is thine,
When hearts divorc'd, bow down at nature's shrine,
They seem to join again, in spirit whole,
And claim the fealty of thy mingled soul—
Some memoried tale—a birthday of the year,
In vain recurring, prompts the secret tear —
Thus on the gale that sweeps along the strings
The mystic harp once more its music flings
In spirit words, thus yearning o'er the past
Æolian winds methinks the cadence cast.

　" Farewell! how sad the word
　" To say whilst thy returning years are young ;
　" Like as a passing bell by traveller heard
　" The daisied meads among.

　" Yet such thy fate and mine,
　" Thou art the mead with daisies sprinkled o'er ;
　" I the lone traveller note the fatal sign
　" That parts us evermore.

" 'Tis Time doth strike the bell ;
" Thou hear'st it not now in thy spring tide day,
" Heedless of merry chime or solemn knell,
" Or who is sad or gay.

" But now, with portents fraught,
" Thy morn departing, hails, for ill or good
" Thy day of life,—and all thou hast been taught,
" Must form thy womanhood.

" Oft hath my yearning soul
" Through darksome hours of long estrangéd years,
" Claimed in my dreams, o'er thee that dear control,
" Affection true reveres.

" O ! if thy lot be glad,
" Because we have not interchang'd our care,
" Take me for friend, who suffer'd and was sad,
" Nor marr'd thy prospect fair.

" But if thy future years
" Be dark and gloomy from the teachings past,
" Take me for foe, who brought thee to thy tears,
" And all thy sorrows cast.

" So if thou hear'st it said—
" Sorrow and I through death have found an end,
" 'Twill be, one earliest enemy is dead,
" Or one unhonor'd friend.

G

" Farewell ! my spirit views
" Thy womanhood and years of doubt are past ;
" Crown'd is my dream, no more e'en hope pursues,
" But yieldeth peace at last.

" Thus,—when before his glass—
" The rapt astronomer with vigil blest—
" Seeing the long-sought star in brightness pass,
" Content, retires to rest.

Now darkly grows the landscape all around,
I faint and falter to the expiring sound,
I wander heedless and my failing sight
Tells I have stray'd to realms of utter night.
No sun, no stars—strange shapes flit to and fro,
Yet onward to yon verge impell'd they go,
Then sink for ever in the gloom profound,
Beyond the slippery rocks which loom around.
Regret and all his minions seem to fade,
And I am wandering to a deeper shade.
Whence is this gloom profound ? and must I trace
The hidden horrors of this dreadful place,
Unharm'd shall I escape the general fate,
These gloomy pilgrims seem but to await,
As travelling with the loads they mutely bear ?
Victims of destiny and grim despair !
From every land they come, and move along
In sullen silence, all that haggard throng ;

By varied roads, this self same path achiev'd,
Come the deceivers and the long deceiv'd.
Here too Conceit walks hopeless and alone
For uncheck'd vauntings he must here atone;
Where none will comfort the unmaskéd cheat—
All equal only in the woes they meet;
Tears are estrang'd—despair hath no retreat.
Vain brawler! he who promiséd so much
In offering shadows not a hand could touch,
Raving of rights—'midst plaudits to prevail—
He named not duties in his fraudful tale.
Eternal rights! no matter what the theme,
Or who may suffer in the wild extreme—
Lost is the power that but a fool excites—
Disgust succeeds a revelry of rights.
Yet driven to this land of dark despair,
He finds his great antagonist is there;
Who driven by faction on a different road,
O'er borne with sorrow seeks despair's abode.
    Yes! here the patriot too, whose truthful voice
Lov'd to address the freemen of his choice,
Scorning the ease which flows from flattery sure,
He dar'd to tell of faults he strove to cure;
Show'd that the heartless pander to the crowd,
Courts easy fame in duties disallow'd,
Oppos'd by faction yet he dar'd to hold
That rights were clear, so duties must be told,

That thus the happy trio, hand-in-hand,
Might walk together proudly through the land—
As scorning wily arts and mask'd pretence,¹
Companions true—rights, duties, common sense.

What mournful tone pervades the sighing wind,
Which not an outlet from this realm can find ;
Where every heart-pang breath'd in days of yore,
Wanders along the dreary spell-bound shore ;
Haunts every spot that echoes to its cry,
The memoried tones of sorrow long gone by.
E'en still I hear—Despair ! as given to thee,
The holy plaint that mov'd Gethsemane—
Or David's hopeless wail, who mourn'd too well
The son rebellious who in treason fell ;
Remembering but the father in the king,
All crimes forgotten in the news they bring—
By death bereav'd,—he mourns a triumph won,
And hath no cry but " Absalom, my son ! "

What pensive pilgrims linger all around
These miry paths that lie through broken ground,
Where not one joy hath grown a tender flower,
Or light of hope illum'd life's transient hour ;
When fled from earth the trusting and the true,
And left but broken hearts expos'd to view ;
These are the silent travellers on the way,
Who look through utter darkness for the day.

Grave of the heart! what power can mortals seek
To aid their need when bitter winds are bleak;
When all unshelter'd from the stormy blast
On life's drear waste their pilgrimage is cast.
Hope far away hath borne his wings of light,
Despair's dark pinions brood o'er lands of night,—
I hear the demon whose wild wind shall sweep
Along this rocky pathway to the deep;
With stormy discord and with fatal breath,
Tempestuous raise a hurricane of death.
Borne to the beetling edge a moment more,
Pensile to cling the dreadful chasm o'er;
The slippery grasp is clench'd at length in air
And all is mute in caverns of despair.
O spirit of the heart! once more I pray
Give me to see of light one little ray.
Save me, great power!—avert this dreadful scene,
Which now surrounds,—in mercy intervene!
Thou who hast heard my call, hear this my cry,
Here from this charnel house—nor let me die!
It comes in thunder! ah! the dreadful crash
That sure must follow on that vivid flash;
A moment's pause—one moment to prepare—
For life's annihilation in despair.
Thou man of Uz! methinks I hear thee now,
When deep affliction darken'd on thy brow,

Here in this gloomy pathway as thou trod,
Sustain'd by thy unfaltering trust in God;
Thy suffering wail yet hovers in the air,
Faith's witness on this passage to despair;
Mock'd by thy friends when thou would'st seek their
    aid,
Thy heart's religion only undismay'd.
Thy faith triumphant shed a holy light
Above despair's dark realms of utter night,
And led thy footsteps to a brighter goal,   .
Faith's high reward—a haven for the soul.

    The war of waters comes from the profound,
I grope my way—I know the awful sound;
I see the rocks that overhang the deep,
Black as the clouds that roll along the steep.
O! may my darken'd footsteps guided be,
Light of the soul! O sun of truth by thee;
O let me yet the heart's religion trace
That hidden land! that true abiding place.

    Hark! through the darkness—on the wind I hear
A choral echo that seems travelling near;
Yes! memory listen!—'tis an old refrain—
It comes! it comes! to rescue me again.
Nearer and nearer breathe the sounds of peace,
I tremble lest despair shall bid them cease.
Hence horrid thought! faith bids the heart defy
His power to rule the kindred of the sky;

Borne on the breeze, though darkness reigns profound
Faith hears each voice, each well remember'd sound,
And thus, in words vouchsaf'd to mortal ear
The spirit voices of the past I hear—

" Pilgrim mortal! curious seeker
" For the things that hidden lie,
" Though we strive not with the weaker
" Each of us hath been a speaker,
" When thy heart would claim reply. ·

" Now thou hast thy journey ended—
" Now we come to ease thy care ;
" Back to life thou shalt be tended,
" For whilst thus thou art befriended,
" Never need'st thou fear despair—

" See yon volume! in its pages,
" All the heart's true history find ;
" All the wisdom of the sages,
" Who have liv'd in bygone ages—
" Thou hast eyes and art not blind.

" All its passions there pourtray'd,
" (And they are for aye the same) ;
" Though at times it be dismay'd,
" Though in pride it be array'd,
" To earth alone it hath a claim.

" Its religion hath no section,
" Sought by thee,—thy search how vain;
" Nature owns its best affection—
" To heav'n belongs its pure subjection,
" And it wears a golden chain.

" All the cavils, all the learning,
" Cannot give a form divine;
" A thousand sects, the truth discerning,
" Each is right when humbly turning
" To the great Creator,—thine.

" Forbear to murmur—there is treasure,
" See before thee lies the whole;
" Thou may'st scan the heart's true measure,
" Know its sorrow and its pleasure,
" And its homage to the soul.

" Now the volume faintly gleaming
" In the darkness of despair,
" Shall guide thee safely from thy dreaming,
" All thy sorrows be but seeming,
" In the hopes that triumph there.

" Back to earth then as thou speedest,
" Not again through paths o'erpast;
" Take the book and as thou readest,
" Find the postern gate thou needest,
" And be grateful to the last."

'Tis mercy's mission, lo! before mine eyes,
Wreath'd with a halo, see a volume lies,
Its pure pale light gives forth a mystic ray,
To show its outline on the miry way;
With gradual power its ray-like glories shine,
Till on the heart it pours a flood divine.
Gone is despair—the stormy terrors cease—
Whilst hope returns,—a messenger of peace;
I seize the volume with its wonders rife,
The Heart's true Chronicle!—the Book of Life!
Guided by light that falls upon my way,
I reach the promised outlet to the day.
I pass the portal, and amaz'd I stand—
Once more in life—again on mortal land,
Suffus'd in tears my aching eyes behold
The open volume with its page of gold;
Dreams of the heart no more my thoughts employ,
Here are its deeds—its sorrow and its joy,
I wake with hope, and all its blessings born,
Proclaim the advent of a glorious morn.
As when Orion, blind at Chios, led
To where the eastern sun just peer'd his head,
His darken'd eyeballs 'neath the morning ray,
Renew'd their wonted light and hail'd the day—
Spell-bound I feel a light divine inspire
My waking thoughts, and feel renascent fire;

With grateful heart I raise my wondering eyes,
Morn's herald beam is in the amber skies!
Lo! Helios quits the golden boat of night,
Form'd by Vulcanus for his eastward flight;
When with his journey round the world opprest,
He gains at length his mansions in the west;
Then sailing back the hemisphere below
Refresh'd he bids again morn's palace glow;
Again he takes the circuit of the skies,
Whilst choral psalms and holy matins rise.
    Beneath this glory of the morning hour,
I bend before interminable power;
Nature puts forth her beauties to impart
The sweet condolences that bless the heart.
Again the hum of life is sounding near,
Again the voices of the past I hear;
I take my pilgrim-staff, and wend my ways,
Chasten'd and prompted by those spirit lays;
Around me smile the hopes of days to come,
Fainter and farther to the final home.
Above is light that conquers black despair,
And seems to paint in hues divine the air,
And with its glory every thought controls
To lead the spirit to the home of souls.

MEMORIES OF MERTON,

(SURREY.)

MEMORIES OF MERTON.

PART FIRST.

MEMORIES OF MERTON.

——: oo :——

DEDICATION.

TO A LADY.

" LONG AGO ! " " long ago ! ! "—'tis the sound of
  the bells—
  How they ring out the ages, those words of the
  soul,
Of " the past," of " the present," of " for ever" the
  knells, ·
  Fresh memories they chime—new mourners they
  toll.
Then, lady, the poet, whose pen and whose heart
  Are tracing the dream-time that onward doth flow,
Would catch just a tone ere those mem'ries depart,
  And sing a refrain of the dear " long ago."

H

Nor to joy, nor to sorrow alone shall the muse
　　Give the dream of the soul or the chords of the
　　　song,
But, meek as the shadow the object pursues,
　　To the sad and the joyous the theme shall belong.
But yet 'tis our nature when backward we gaze
　　On the scenes we are leaving and ne'er more may
　　　know,
Like lov'd hearts departed, we cherish those days,—
　　Rememb'ring but good of the dear " long ago."

Nor should we so mingle the dust of the past
　　With the sunshine of mem'ry that then was our
　　　own,—
We had but the dream that was long before cast,
　　And scenes which from others for ever had flown.
And thus in the future—though chang'd be the scene
　　That mem'ry recalls in its lingering flow,
There are hearts looking onward, like those that
　　　have been,
　　Like us, they shall dream of a dear " long ago."

"Long ago!" " long ago!!"—oh, 'tis music divine;
　　If our hearts are unsullied old Time is our friend;
The pilgrims of truth he leads on to the shrine,
　　Where memory in worship for ever shall bend.

Then, lady, believe not the days yet to be,
  Deep shadows o'er memory ever can throw,
The sunshine departed, how sweetly we see
  The calm moonlight rays of the dear "long ago."

MEMORIES OF MERTON.

(SURREY.)

————:oo:————

PART 1.

INTRODUCTION—MERTON ROAD—THE WATERFALL—COLLIER'S

WOOD—SINGLE GATE—PERSONAL REMINISCENCES.

———

THE watch-dog in the blaze of day,
Half sleeping 'neath the solar ray,
Scarce notes the sounds that meets his ear,
Or even footsteps hovering near.
But when the sun grows red and low,
And western skies begin to glow,
No sounds escape his eager care,
Whilst sight and sense their duties share;
And, till those sounds are borne away,
The welkin echoes with his bay.

So MERTON, when in days gone by
I saw thee 'neath life's mid-day sky,
Nor deem'd that change could come so soon,
And I should gaze in afternoon ;
Whilst suns arose and set again,
I slept and dream'd upon my chain.
But now the evening clouds arise,
And moonbeams flood the twilight skies,
I hear the sounds of change, and see
The harbingers of destiny
With stranger footsteps steal along
Thy bowers, ere yet the poet's song
Hath told the tale that thou wert fair,
Or sung of other days that were.
Thus, could I raise a clarion tone,
My faithful trumpet-call when blown,
Should echo o'er each wood and dell,
The tones of Memory's sentinel.
For hark ! I hear the ringing click,
The vigorous trowel cleaves the brick,
And tells me the beleaguering foes
Just halt around thee ere they close,
And circle in one vast embrace
The things that were,—nor leave a trace,
Save what the memory, or the bard
May rescue from cold disregard.

Thus, in the semblance of the past
Things live again in fiction cast:—
As we have seen the hoary pile,
Blacken'd with ages, gleam and smile,
When art has drench'd the walls, and made
Old Time restore the tribute paid;
In fancy then awhile we gaze
On the new work of olden days,
And as the subtle beauties show,
Emerging to the cleansing flow,
We see with our forefathers' eyes,
And feel once more their ecstasies.
So to the poet's love shall seem
The early image of his dream,
Chang'd though it be, his loving heart
Would rather be deceiv'd than part;
And though he cannot hope renew
As in the days he worshipp'd true,
Would claim no love from present things,
But, as imagination flings
Its incense o'er the spirit-dream,
Would only ask that they should *seem;*
Content that change should never rise
In ghostly facts before his eyes,
Nor crave, for sake of reason fair
To see the chang'd things as they are,

But rather dream, as once he dream'd,
They seeming, too, as once they seem'd.
Then MERTON, thou to me once more
Shalt come from dreamland as of yore ;
As gazing through the mists of years,
Each storied moment reappears ;
I see thy road unchang'd and still,
Descending Tooting's gentle hill,
The narrow defile leads the way,
And I am dreaming in the day.

Behold the humble chapel's space,
Small, but enough for special grace ;
Though many may be called, 'tis true
Th' elect are but a chosen few ;
And if we judge the building's scope,
There's little room for growing hope.

I now the gradual slope recall,
That usher'd in the waterfall,
Which seem'd a prelude fair and good
To vocal shades of Collier's Wood ;—*
Lovely, when Spring-time's fantasies
With varnish'd cones had deck'd the trees,
And when the topmost branches bore
The choir of rooks from days of yore.

---

* Collier's Wood, between Tooting and Merton, used to be
amous for its rookery.

Lovely, when Summer crown'd the scene
With golden tresses 'twin'd with green ;
And air that rivall'd eastern climes,
Toy'd with the flowers, and swept the limes.
Lovely, when Autumn heap'd her store,
And varied robes in moonlight wore.
When the full orb in mellow prime
Flooded with gold the harvest time.
And lovely, too, when Winter's reign
Restor'd the crystal shapes again,
With silvery fancies—frosted gems
To deck a thousand diadems.
Thus usher'd in the village lay,
And Nature kindly led the way.
Now as I claim a ray from thee,
Light of the Muse !—Mnemosyne !
I pray thee, that again may pass
Each by-gone scene before thy glass,
And give again a glimpse to me
From out thy stores of Memory.
Though oft the humble scene and sport
Where simple joy and health resort—
Are worthy of the burning page,
The chronicle from age to age—
Yet thou hast only power to trace
What Time too surely will efface,

As living votaries pass away
New worshippers appear and pray.
Thus thou dost hold thy genial plan
To lengthen out the life of man.
Thou dost not dally long with Fate
But deeds of story—things of state—
To History thou dost relegate.
Then Memory breathe thy mystic air,
O let me see them as they were,
The club that boasted funny rule,*
The village clown†—but half a fool,
The social villagers recall,
And let me view them one and all.

    What sees the spirit?—hurrying by
In stately speed and panoply;
Sure Memory doth illusion bring!
For see it is a moving thing!
The well-appointed coach appears
Emerging from the by-gone years,
As through the gate it wends its way
With living freight of olden day.

---

   * "The Funny Club" and "Social Villagers" were gatherings for amateur acting and singing.

   † Merton, like most villages, had its eccentric ne'er-do-well, sometimes clever enough to do without hard work.

The coachman and the horses, too,
The well-remember'd usual few,
There, join'd in chat, they while away
The hour that parts them for the day.
The lawyer sits in quiet state
As if he would anticipate
The great decision of the day,
And all the part he has to play.
There, too, I see the factory lord,
Whisp'ring his neighbour many a word;
And now speaks out in right good will
The merchant prince* of Cannon Hill.
Yes! all seem present as I gaze
Through Memory's vista to those days.

  Ah! now again the scene grows bright
As various changes spring to light.
This memoried spot—the turnpike gate—
Recalls the hours of by-gone fate;
The scenes of anxious strife it knew,
When rival guards their post-horns blew†
And woke the echoes far and near
With summons of the charioteer,

---

* The late wealthy Richard Thornton, Esq.

† Many years ago there was a great omnibus opposition at Merton, which lasted a considerable time, and caused much interest and excitement.

That made the gossips gather round
The rival coaches at the sound,
And peopled all these quiet roads
To see the startings and the loads.

No more the scene—no more the strife,
We pass the gate in quiet life,
And noting many a souvenir
Of things achiev'd in pleasure here,
The dream-spell clothes the varying scene
And hours return as they have been.
The singers and musicians, too,
The past recall—the scenes renew;
The dancers come again and seem
Deck'd, as of old, in fancy's dream;
Their faces all unchang'd and bright
With expectation and delight.
And, O! the actors! come not they
In all their improvis'd array?
Yes! they are here,—the play! the play!
In a delirium trip along
The dance, the acting, and the song;
Old Time is cheated, for his glass
Is chok'd by sands that will not pass.

I dare not listen, for my brain
Grows mad with every old refrain,
The spectre music dies away,
And all is gone, and all is day.

Hence, ideal woe! and things that seem ;
Yonder there flows a haunted stream ;
Shall we, to wake the sleeping past,
That has o'er all its mantle cast,
Now turn aside the bridge beyond,
To raise again illusion fond?
Sweet Wandle, hail! 'neath yonder arch
Thou sweepest on thy forcéd march,
As if the hours of pleasure gone
Had slipp'd, and left thee all alone,
And thou hadst donn'd thy travelling guise
All hurried from thy deep surprise—
With headlong dash thy fervour gives,
Resolved to catch the fugitives.
Pause we awhile, ere yet thy speed
Is check'd, that we ourselves may read ;
Thou dost but hurry to the stream
That tears thee from thy source and dream.
So we, who striving to o'ertake
Lost hours, lost hopes, for memory's sake,
Like thee may seek the long-lost thing,
And find, too late, our following.
  Well! thou may'st pause and take thy dream,
For here thou wert an elfin stream,
And well thou dreamest in thy flow
Thou hast o'erta'en the " long ago.'

Here, on thy daisied banks, were seen
The bright-ey'd nymphs and fairy queen ;
Here Naiads in the moonlight stray'd,
And mortal longings oft betray'd ;
Whilst listening raptured to the strain
Of Philomel with vocal train.
Elfin and mortal own'd the spell,
And Time went on—but mark'd them well ;
Though whispers fell to breezy sighs,
Though gliding forms and glancing eyes
Sought on thy banks the Naiad's bowers,
And charm'd the meretricious hours,
Yet, now, methinks, thou may'st speed on,
Thy swains are old, thy Naiads gone ;
Though yet thy waters dance and gleam,
Though yet the mill is on thy stream,
E'en though the miller, unbeguil'd,
Remains unchangéd—Memory's child !*
Yet now Romance hath strode away
And all thy vistas cloth'd in grey.
When Naiads, tir'd of elfin lives,
Chang'd long ago to mortal wives,
Who, mingled with life's heartless throng,
Heed not thy minstrel, or his song.

---

* The Flour Mill, Wandle Bank, Merton, has been for many
years in the possession of Messrs. Child.

Then haste thee, Wandle! speed thy course,
Thy wavelets sparkling quit thy source;
How gay thy mirror'd bubbles run
And leap, like dolphins in the sun,
From Beddington in many a vein
To Carshalton through park and plain;
In many a guise the poet sees
Thy varying forms and memories;
Retarded oft by dam and mill,
Thou seem'st to pause like giant still,
Who, check'd a little in his path,
Breathes, just a moment, in his wrath,
Then, with a bound, o'erleaps the bar,
And thunders on his way afar.

MEMORIES OF MERTON.

PART SECOND.

MEMORIES OF MERTON,

(SURREY.)

————:oo:————

PART SECOND.

HISTORY, THE DEPOSITORY OF MEMORIES—MERTON ABBEY;
HISTORICAL COMBINATIONS CONNECTED WITH IT—THE
VILLAGE—LORD NELSON—THE OLD CHURCH—CONCLUSION

————

Mortality! how short thy flight!
How gay thy noon, and deep thy night,
What meteor-visions startle thee,
And shake thy throne of memory?
Thy little all of sense and power
Is dwindled to an insect's hour,
And all that thou canst give to fame
Is but a soon-forgotten name.

    Yet there are memories bright and high,
That will not fade, that cannot die,

Written in storied life sublime,
The kings, and not the slaves of time;
There, all enthron'd, doth·memory live,
And stores the records life may give.

If ancient wisdom give the tale
That shall o'er changeful Time prevail,
Her walls e'en yet from ruin free,
Where learned worth found sanctuary;
If deeds of daring on the main
Heroes recall to life again;
Or History's bright recording page
Illumine many an after age,
Then MERTON, thou shalt ever claim
Thy record on the rolls of Fame,
And blend thy past—thy scenes of ease
With Britain's proudest memories.

See where the flinty walls around
Tell of the ancient classic ground,
Where holy men, in days of yore,
In teachings of religious lore,
Gave to the world those precepts bright
Which shed o'er thee a holy light.
Methinks I see their cloistered cells,
And matins hear—and vesper bells;
And, lingering to the storm of Time,
Which stay'd the worship—hush'd the chime,

Arise to find relentless trade
Now claims the wreck that Time hath made.
E'en yet these walls in pride maintain
The ancient bounds of Faith's domain,
When war and violence alone
Could rule the world or keep a throne—
The Abbey, when the strife did cease,
Could teach the gentler arts of peace.

Though ancient days, long past and gone,
Saw first its walls arise in stone,
Yet, long before, the fabric stood
A thing of solid worth in wood.
Such, the first Henry—wise and brave,
The manor to the Norman gave,
Who rais'd the stone-built pile at length,
And after-ages own'd its strength.
O! what a mighty power it saw,
When Rome to princes gave the law;
When many a conqueror, duty led,
Before the mitre bow'd his head.
Though ravag'd kingdoms own'd the might
Of warrior-king and mailèd knight—
E'en he who bore his standard free,
In fields of France and Normandy—
The second Henry—England's lord,
Whose hand victorious wav'd the sword,

And who, whilst conquering every foe,
Yet sank beneath domestic woe,
And though in nature stern and rude,
Died of his child's ingratitude,
Even he, to priestly rule a foe,
And 'gainst the Church who dealt a blow,
Yet at a'Becket's tomb he knelt
Whilst prior and monks their penance dealt :
E'en warlike Henry bore the blows
From priests he would not brook from foes

But, MERTON, hark ! for time recalls
The sounds of joy around thy walls.
England's third Henry seeks thee now,
To place a crown upon his brow ;
Though no new honours grace his name,
He brings, in pomp, his royal dame,
And, in thy Abbey's sacred light,
His oath to swear—his faith to plight.

Here, MERTON, to thy Abbey came,
In all the panoply of fame,
From Palestine and Normandy,
The banner'd knights of chivalry ;—
All on one errand duly met,
To aid the young Plantagenet.
Here came the King, on counsel bent
With Abbot-Lords of Parliament.

Here laws were issued from thy halls,*
Which linger yet around thy walls;
And though Time's fingers tear away
Each vestige of the olden day,
That thou wert great in days gone by,
Is fame, where truth will never die—
And History tells to ages far,
In peace thou nurs'd the sons of war.
Thence every age from thee would claim
Thy teachings for a future fame,
And all thy holy influence sought
To shape the embryo realm of thought;
Till the last Henry's ruthless hand
Destroy'd thy homestead—took thy land,
But could not raze those walls to dust—
Firm as thy faith's eternal trust—
They yet withstood the trying day,
To wait on Time's more sure decay.
And even down to modern tale,
Thy strength did Cromwell's men avail,
And thus thy storied pomp and state
Departed at the word of Fate,

---

* It is said that amongst the "Statutes of Merton," enacted
in the reign of Henry III., was the well-known "Statute of
Mortmain," now existing.

As if to crush thy primal plan,
And mock thee with the Puritan—
Thy walls, though sheltering, frown'd upon
The Roundhead soldiers' garrison.*

Now, MERTON, whilst I strike the string,
And warlike deeds and valour sing,
Ere yet I change the chord, and wake
A sweeter theme, for peace's sake,
To sing, as now before me rise,
Thy storied great, or memoried wise ;
I dare not let the impassion'd theme
Float all away on Lethe's stream,
Without recalling once again
The ancient tone for modern strain,
Which, worthy of chivalric days,
Should sound Fame's trumpet-note of praise.

England ! thou homestead of the free,
From ancient days of chivalry,
To memory's past and present hour
Thy varied monuments of power
Proclaim that wisdom—valour—truth,
Are honor'd with perennial youth ;

---

* A Parliamentary army garrisoned Merton Abbey at the time
of the Civil War.

That, in thy sepulchre of fame,
Sleeps, but ne'er fades, the precious name.
O! could the muse but singly take
Each storied tomb—its history wake,
Where London's great cathedral shows
Its sheltered heroes—friends and foes;—
In vain the task—but 'midst the throng
That moves through time each poet's song,
Thy tomb, Horatio,* e'er shall be
The theme for Merton's memory.

 When lovely Peace had spread her wing,
And hush'd the battle's thundering,
The wearied nation sought repose,
And shut the Janus of its woes.
Dear MERTON! in thy home of calm,
Thy Nelson sought the healing balm ;
Hop'd, in thy pleasant vale of streams,
To bask in beauty's smiling beams.
Though yet he heard its mutterings far
The storm had pass'd and hush'd the war.
In vain the peaceful tokens seen ;
In vain the dances on the green ;
In vain the joy-bells welcome home
The hardy crews from Ocean's foam.

---

* Lord Nelson, who had a seat at Merton.

Again the tocsins sound alarms,
Though lovers sigh, the nation arms,
And from his village once again
Goes forth the thunderer of the main.
Weep, MERTON, weep again those tears
That fell from thee in by-gone years,
Whene'er the tale be ponder'd o'er
How Nelson saw thy shades no more ;
But as Trafalgar's Cape drew near,
Whose bay should close his bright career,
Though glory gave a victor's crown—
Though history echoes his renown—
Yet on the nation fell a blow,
And, MERTON, thou,—the home of woe,
Could bring the brave heart back no more
That lov'd so well the British shore.

See, where in London towering stands
The column'd statue worth demands,
How guarded by the emblems fair
Of Britain's lion, watching there,
He seems to scan the world afar,
And scent the scenes of olden war ;
And though he range o'er tower and dome
Seems gazing on his village home,
As if his latest watch should be
For ever, MERTON, fix'd on thee ;

And, lingering o'er life's last farewell,
'Midst ruin'd halls he lov'd so well,
He seems to chide the wayward fate
That left his bowers all desolate.
  So falls, in storm, the forest oak,
But Time can ne'er its fame revoke ;
So die the violet and the rose,
But memory gives them sweet repose ;
So fade in air the dreamy tones
That music gives and memory owns,
Bringing to life the spirit strain,
With every tear and joy again.
  Yet it shall be that humbler things
Shall rise to fame on memory's wings ;
And though the acacia's grace we see,
Love's emblem shall the myrtle be ;
Nor shall the daisy's starry eye,
That seems to watch the evening sky,
Withdraw that steady upward gaze
Beneath the sun's meridian blaze ;
So, though the hero of the seas,
Lives in our hearts and memories,
And noble deeds shall ever be
All sacred to posterity,
We own the rights of peaceful fame,
When science gilds a humble name.

Then seek the church's ancient walls,
Where many a monument recalls
The noble worth of Merton's dead
Who live in deeds remembered;
And many a record shall be found
Within the wallèd burial ground,
To tell of worthy skill and deed,
That many an age, well-pleas'd, may read.
And though the Abbey's storied shade
Doth hold the sons of busy trade,
How great the man who perfects art,
And aids the trophies of the mart.
So, Nixon,* to thy praise is lent
The record of thy monument.
Thou gav'st the Merton printers' will
The perfect offspring of thy skill,
And after ages own that thou
Art worthy of remembrance now.

   Yes! here again doth memory stay
To linger o'er the by-gone day;
For here the poet may not pass
† That humble rail—those mounds of grass,

---

  * Nixon, who effected great improvements in calico printing, has a monument in Merton Churchyard.

  † Three of my children, with their maternal grandfather, are buried here.

Without recalling hours of yore,
And all the sorrows that they bore.
The pangs are gone !—but memory weeps
Where each dear by-gone image sleeps.
How sweet to me this hallow'd ground,
For hope, with memory, gazing round
Where babes, and grandsire, sleep in clay,
Sees vision'd meetings far away.

But now, ere yet we quit the spot
Where memory lives—where pride is not ;
How passing strange—yon long record *
Of sorrow with its lengthened word,
That tells, redundantly, the bliss
Of union in a world like this,
And strives to show a tender claim
In verse which echoes back the name.
Methinks it tells a tale too long
Of grief that is not deep, but strong,
That with its first delirium o'er
May find a solace known before,
And with the sorrow all express'd
The letters prolix stand confess'd,

---

* A stone just inside the church ground has a somewhat lengthy
and peculiar inscription.

Which readers see, nor sighs refuse,
But think on Gray's " unletter'd muse.* "
 I quit thee, MERTON,—lingering too
Recede thy homesteads from my view,
For here the school I see again,
The very children in the lane
Seem to have waited through the years,
To form the tableau that appears,
Just as of old, they listless stray
Uncertain in their wonted play ;
Endymion, waking from his sleep,
Each likeness in his mind would keep.
 MERTON, farewell ! thy foes around
Are closing o'er thy memoried ground ;
Thy olden signs they seek to crush,
And meet thee even in thy " Rush.† "
Their step is onward—close at hand,
All gone the fields of Thornton's land,
And dare, ere long, more desperate still,
To brave his home—his Cannon Hill.
The " Leather Bottle," old in name,
I dare not hope to find the same,

---

 * " Their names, their years, spelt by th' unletter'd muse,
  The place of fame and elegy supply."—GRAY.

 † Merton Rush, wherein stands the " Old Leather Bottle " Inn
is at the extremity of the village.

As in the days it form'd the bound
Of Merton in that little round,
But the foe thy fields upon,
From Morden and from Wimbledon
They hurrying come, in serried ranks,
In front and rear, on both thy flanks;
And when the victory is achiev'd,
And thy existence disbeliev'd,
In all that made thee once excel
Let history then the doubt dispel;
In all that made thee once so lov'd,
By memory be the doubt disprov'd,
Thy poet's song be always young,
To show thou wert both lov'd and sung.
How lov'd!—thy waters ceaseless flow
The answer give, that it was so—
As, moving every landscape through,
Thy stream, like life, is ever new,
And, gathering love in length'd range,
Went joyous on nor heeded change.
How sung!—ah me! in time to come
Say that thy poet sang of home;
Say that the sun of life rose high
And show'd a bright unclouded sky;
Say that he knew of wealth no share,
But hope, divine, dispell'd his care—

Hope, fann'd by every loving breeze
That comes from spirit-ecstasies.
And then, though gone the minstrel be,
Say, MERTON, that he sung of thee,
And Time, whilst ringing out thy knell,
Shall sound from his responsive bell
Thy poet's sigh—" Farewell, FAREWELL."

OCCASIONAL PIECES.

TO MRS. SMITH,

(FORMERLY MISS BARTRAM,)

ON HER MARRIAGE, OCT. 16th, 1867.

———

A poet's wreath, by fancy wrought,
   A garland thou may'st truly wear,
When bridal flowers no more are sought
   To deck the sunlight of thy hair.

I bring to thee—ne'er may'st thou spurn
   The loving precepts of its truth ;
Cherish'd through life, it will return,
   For aye thy coronal of youth.

And he who is a King to-day
   Shall prize the queenly diadem,
That casts o'er life a gentler ray
   Than gleams from Beauty's sparkling gem.

Though blended strangely it may be,
  Thy kindly heart will not refuse
The emblems of thy life and thee,
  And woven with all truthful hues.

For here the " Bridal rose " doth blend
  With " Bluebell " and its constancy,
That happy love may never end
  Whilst Time doth mingle flowers for thee.

Now bind thy garland round with " Fern,"
  The scarlet " Fuschia," too, we'll find ;
For taste hath chosen to discern
  Its emblem in this floweret kind.

A rosy garland it shall be,
  For thou should'st have thy true reward ;
And virtue owns thy loyalty,
  And crowns thee with a rich regard.

With " Hawthorn buds " will Spring renew
  Each hope thou hast this day reveal'd ;
Love's " Myrtle " may no tears bedew,
  Nor faith's strong " Ivy " be conceal'd.

The " Guelder roses " come at length,
  And gladden still the vale of age ;
The setting sun, with failing strength,
  Yet gilds life's happy pilgrimage.

Immortal joys these flowers shall show,
  Nor shall their beauties e'er depart ;
In thy soul's garden may they grow,
  And weave a chaplet round thy heart.

To faith's pure altar then repair,
  For love o'erpays the sacrifice—
Can make the wild a sweet parterre,
  The humblest home a paradise.

"THE FADED OLD SHAWL."

I see thee again—like the spectre of years
  Long gone to their rest—all faded and dead,
Like a rainbow (poor child of bright sunshine and
      tears,)
  So palest thou now with the days that have fled.

Oh! gently unfold it; for voices I hear
  From its dust of decay—living motes of the
      past—
That tell of the form that no more shall appear,
  And the hopes of the heart, too precious to last.

Though slumbering now, thou canst not forget
  How near *then* thou wert to the throbs of her
      heart—
Canst tell of emotions that felt no regret,
  Of sighs that alone could devotion impart.

Then say, in thy mystic voice, sleeper of years !
When round her thy fabric she daintily drew,
Was there faith in her sigh ? was there love in her
    tears ?
Was she selfish or vain ? erratic or true ?

Thy gloomy, worn aspect responses reveal ;
In thy moth-eaten structure I note thy reply ;
For deceit or decay can no art e'er conceal,
And loves, like the roses, must wither and die.

Then back to thy grave ! thy presence forbear ;
I sigh o'er the sorrows thy teachings impart ;
Too often, like thee, mortals yield in despair,
To die like thyself, with a worm at the heart.

ON RECEIVING

A REMONSTRATIVE LETTER

FROM A VALUED FRIEND,

AND WHICH LETTER EXCEEDED THE WEIGHT ALLOWED TO THE POSTAL STAMP IT BORE.

———

I got a letter from a friend,
    As kind a friend as e'er could be,
Who in her missive did intend
    Some slight reproof to send to me,
But with such gravity o'erweighted,
It could not pass as *under-rated*.

And clever is she ? I may say
    That there are very, very few
Whose pen or wit would not betray
    (If they had her's) the stocking blue.
But here *she* fail'd, and (*blue* or *red*)
Outbalanc'd quite her *single head*.

When " heavy matter " we've on hand,
  We cannot mould it to our will,
But, like slow servants, stare and stand—
  The laggard " pages "—boding ill ;
Then to the ground, oft in my rage,
I've " dash'd my *buttons* "—and *the page.*

'Tis said that eyes were given to all,
  Or, if not *all*, at least to most,
That we may stumble not nor fall,
  But *save our heads against a post.*
Now my dear friend has proved instead,
The post would not receive *her head.*

A " man of letters " told me this—
  Not with a view my heart to damp—
That though the text was not amiss,
  It should have borne a higher stamp.
I could not let him prove his view,
My face *alone bore stamp of blue.*

However, as I read it o'er,
  And found its reasonings should prevail,
Its weight, now valued all the more,
  Did balance well life's social scale.
So never fear my heart to move ;
Such *weight and measure* I approve.

THE FICKLE TITANIA.

When Oberon, the King of Fairies, strove
To baffle fair Titania's selfish love,
He on her eyes the amorous dew did press,
And dreamy spells from " Love in idleness."
She woke, to lavish all her tender sighs
On the first creature that should meet her eyes.
By wilful Puck, upon her pathway led,
Appeared a suitor with an ass's head ;
Smitten with tender passion, she adored
The long-ear'd lover as her bosom's lord ;
Nor does it seem recorded by the bard
What colour was the ass of her regard ;
Perhaps by Shakespeare it was kindly done
To prove that rapt Titania sought but one.

Not so the fair Titania of my theme,
With " Love in idleness " a constant dream.
She, in the warmth of youthful hours oppress'd,
A simple one with ass's head caress'd ;

Oft in her willing lap he laid it down,
And wondering gazers saw the head was brown.
Anon some elfin changed her fickle taste,
She doted on another one in haste ;
Black was the head—no demon's could surpass—
In fact he was a most infernal ass.
Amazed, each gazer went his wondering way,
But to return and find the head was grey.
Immortal fairy ! lift thy spell-bound brow,
Declare what head it is thou'rt fondling now.

ON HEARING THE REMARK,

"THERE'S A SKELETON IN EVERY HOUSE."

'Tis said there is a secret smart
   Each mortal dreads to muse upon,
A subtle grief in every heart,
   " In every house a skeleton."

But what it proves is merely this:
   That Time brings griefs and cares to all,
That earth is not our home of bliss,
   And we must bear the earthly thrall.

'Tis not for man to choose aright,
   Nor woman to avoid the bane,
Unless protected by the might
   Of Him who hears no prayer in vain.

How can it be that wayward hearts
   Shall, unprotected, foil the foe,
Who hurls around his poison'd darts,
   And mocks the tortures of our woe.

Yet stay; there may be those whose lives
   Are coldly pois'd 'twixt good and ill,
And never heed who sinks or thrives,
   Nor love, nor hate, beyond their skill.

Who never risk an aching heart,
   But, calmly looking life around,
Will bear for none a suffering part,
   Nor by Love's bitter laws be bound.

'Tis well for them, if such there be,
   That thus 'midst strife can keep so cool;
But such exceptions seem to me
   To show our case, and prove the rule.

Then let us bear with tranquil mind
   The weeds that grow amidst our flowers,
And take the comfort we may find—
   There must be sorrow worse than ours.

LAVENDER.

SUGGESTED BY RECEIVING SOME OF THE BLOOM.

———

" Where goest thou ? " a minstrel said
   To eager youth he met in joy ;
Love on his eyes his hand had laid,
   So he, half-blinded, chased the boy.

" I seek Love's fragrant Lavender,
   " To smitten hearts a sweet content ;
" For it doth yield in scented air
   " Love's proudest boon—acknowledgment.

" How dear it is to truly love,
   " And gladly wear a mystic chain ;
" But dearer far the bliss to prove,
   " Whilst loving, I am lov'd again."

" Stay," said the minstrel ; " caution take,
   " Nor rashly win the fragrant prize
" Which yields its perfume for thy sake,
   " Yet danger often underlies.

" My sires would sing, in bardish rhymes,
  "How, 'neath the plant's sweet covert shade,
" The viper asp in olden times
  " Coil'd round the root in ambuscade.

" Danger attendant ever there,
  " ' Distrust ' they nam'd the fragrant plant,
" Lest Beauty's bloom, with fatal snare,
  " Might ruin whom it should enchant.

" 'Tis but a fable ; but take heed—
  " It is of value great to thee ;
" For in the olden tale we read
  " Love's lifetime and Truth's simile.

" Oh ! there are dangers which beset
  " The beauteous beings that inthral
" Man's heart, as in a silken net,
  " Whate'er the fate that may befall.

" The fragrance loving words reveal,
  " Breath'd on the heart in passion's joy,
" Too often serves but to conceal
  " The viper lurking to destroy.

" O fascinating asp!—bright gold!
  " Oft beauty to thine influence kneels ;
" Love lingers in thy shadow cold,
  " With bleeding heart that never heals.

" As at the lov'd one's worshipp'd shrine
  " The trusting heart, with tender gaze,
" Adoring seeks his hope divine,
  " To brighten all his fleeting days.

" Lo! at the base, with venom'd fangs,
  " The selfish reptile specious lies,
" To triumph in the bitter pangs
  " And tears which dim Affection's eyes.

" Then, youth, bethink thee ; but if Time
  " Bestows on Faith its guerdon sweet,
" Take thou the minstrel's simple rhyme,
  " And con it in Love's calm retreat.

" Behold within this little net
  " The gathered bloom of long ago,
" Yielding its primal fragrance yet,
  " Its simple lesson but to show.

" 'Tis love immortal! prov'd and pure,
  " No time can quench its hidden fires;
" By Faith preserv'd, it doth endure,
  " Though life's bright noon in night retires.

" It casts its perfume all around—
  " 'Tis the one spirit hovering near;
" When hearts are bow'd in grief profound,
  " Its hopeful incense checks the tear.

" It rises ever in its bloom,
  " Undying—though in seeming death—
" Imprison'd in its needful tomb,
  " It permeates with welcome breath.

" So shall our love, by Time unmov'd,
  Retain its blessed influence too,
" And in firm trust—acknowledged—proved,
  " In this sweet herb find image true."

   *   *   *   *

The eager youth hath long been gone,
  The simple lay is sung in vain;
And, e'en before the song is done,
  The minstrel stands alone again.

A BYGONE.

—

Seek we to know the future lot
    That Time hath yet within his store,
To aid our joys or charm us not,
    How vain the effort more and more!
But oh ! how dear to you and me
    The unforgotten bygone years,
Could we recall our destiny,
    Nor yield the tribute of our tears !

Could we reverse the mystic roll,
    And turn its foldings back again,
Retrace the writing of the scroll—
    Records of memory's joy and pain ;
With rapid fingers would be past
    The darksome days when youth did wane,
When love estrang'd, in fetters cast,
    Spurn'd silken bond for golden chain.

Beneath th' unrolling of the scroll
  Would fairy things come forth once more,
And many a treasure that we stole
  Reveal its furtive charm of yore ;
Roses would come to scent the way,
  And violets in their olden hue
Would bring again life's memoried day,
  When thou to me wert young and true.

Back would return the loving hours—
  The greenwood ramble, sunny dells ;
Remember'd years of sweetest flowers
  Would cheat our eyes with magic spells.
I, thus forgetting days of age—
  As o'er the enchanting scenes we hung—
In tears would pray that every page
  Should e'er inscribe thee true and young.

TO MY WIFE'S MOTHER

ON HER 80th BIRTHDAY.

(Since Deceased, May 21st, 1872, Aged 83.)

'Tis said that Time hath one sweet task,
   Which stretches o'er a century's space—*
A flower, in many a sun to bask,
   In many a snow to veil its grace,
Whilst bloom and fade the grand and gay
In its one long unbroken day.

'Tis a sweet fable that this flower
   Blooms but so rarely to the eye ;
·It doth but slowly wait its hour,
   When chasten'd 'neath a frigid sky ;
But, grown in regions of the sun,
Its blooming course is quickly run.

In thee—the aloe—then, my friend,
   May Time yet prove the fable true,
Thy temper'd mind, e'en to the end,
   May calm bright skies each day renew—
A bloom each birthday hope bestow,
A hundred years but prove it so.

---

* It is a popular idea that the American aloe blooms but once in a hundred years.

LORD MAYOR'S DAY, 1869.

SCENE : GRESHAM STREET.—*A Girl viewing the Procession from a Window.*

The pageant is passing,—she gazes without,
And lists to the music, and voices that shout;
She sees not the past in the grandeur and blaze,
Nor the splendours and triumphs of chivalric days.
Her eyes sparkle bright,—not a cloud on her brow,
For what should intrude on her innocence now ?
I lift up the wine-cup and sigh o'er its brink,
'Tis a pledge from the heart, and in silence I drink.

So young and so beautiful, gleaming in light,
Like a form in a dream as she blends with the
    sight;
In fancy the lists of the gay tournament
Are rang'd 'neath her eyes as the lances are bent,

Whilst the nodding of plumes, and the din, and the
stir,
Now seem like the homage of knighthood to her ;
She wakes to no mem'ries—'tis too early for
sighs—
No cloud hath yet pass'd o'er the light of her eyes.

Though suns that are gone in our glasses now glow,
Though the past on our hearts may its witcheries
throw,
'Tis the grape—long since turn'd into glorious
wine,
Shall alone to the past prompt a bumper of
mine ;
For love can grow cold and yet mem'ry remain,
All dark and forlorn as it comes o'er the brain ;
I turn down my cup from the sadness of years,
Nor quaff from a goblet so blended with tears.

Then pledge not to memories—clouds of the brain !
The fair and the false—the sordid and vain,
That woke up the love-spell, then mock'd our
delight—
As we see them again in our dreamings of night.

Hence banish the thought that from sorrow would
    rise,
Beauty's Queen here in youth ! let us drink to her
    eyes.
If the old will obtrude on this rapture of mine—
Raise the goblet again to the oldest—of wine.

Still gaily it passes—still onward they come,
Sweet melodies mingle the crash of the drum,
My fancy hath rightly the tournament seen,
She sits in the love-joust of beauty the queen.
They shall strive in the lists and shall sigh in the
    strife,
'Tis a guerdon of love for the battle of life—
Who wins her pure heart hath a trophy as bright
As ever mov'd noble, or dazzled a knight.

Ah, youth of the future ! O thou who shalt share
Her morning of roses—her evening of care,
Let honour and love be the spell of thy youth,
And age shall be crown'd with the chaplet of truth.
Thy pains shall be sooth'd—thy pleasures untold—
The guelder-rose bloom like the June-rose of old,
And the god of the vine with his berries so red,
Shall fling in thy cup all the glories they shed.

Bright floweret of hope ! of morrows in store !
I bid thee farewell, I may see thee no more,
I take thy soft hand—from the scene as thou'rt led,
Though the pageant is done, there's a spell in its
    stead ;
Let me break the enchantment thy beauty hath
    wrought
To serve thee in days when its magic is sought ;
Then know thou, though beauty in splendour may
    shine,
'Tis the truth of the heart that makes beauty
    divine.

TO MY DAUGHTER, MARY,

ON THE DEATH OF HER CHILD, JUNE, 1870.

Come, weeping mother! back to life again
    Revert thine eyes;
Death, the kind conqueror of mortal pain,
    Doth not chastise,
But, clad in angel-garb, he bears away
Thy earthly treasure with a form of clay,
From night's control to brightest day,
          For ever!

Thou'lt not mistrust the accents of my verse,
    For thou dost know
Thy father's heart did bitterly rehearse
    Thy scene of woe.
In days long gone, unpitying Death did claim
Thy childhood's brother and thy father's name:
Despite thy mother's tears, he came
          To sever!

And thou, like us, shalt know the better part,
  Nor dare rebel,
As Time doth weave around thy grateful heart
  A holy spell ;
Then shalt thou grieve no more, but say,
" Thy will be done," (nor far the day,)
Thou'lt not recall the things of clay,
      O never !

TO A LADY,

ON HER RECENT BEREAVEMENT, AND WITH REFERENCE TO
AN OBSERVATION IN HER LETTER, THAT THOUGH WRITING
ONLY ON BUSINESS SHE WAS "WRITING IN TEARS."

———

Tears! ye are bitter, when the soul is sad ;
  When memory, brooding o'er the solemn past,
Doth bring the bygone but in sables clad,
  On sunny banks of yore a shade to cast.
But ye are sweet, when from bright summits fall
  Joy's dewy rills from eyelids of unrest,
When sleepless memories wandering recall
  Life's loving hours with hopes eternal blest.

Tears! ye are graceless, when the wounded heart
  Would summon all the majesty it knows
To bid the false, though dearly lov'd, depart,
  Without a witness to its maddening woes.
But ye are welcome, when the o'ercharged grief
  Fills up the chalice of the aching eyes ;
Sweet are your missions, angels of relief !
  That fall in dews, and then on sunbeams rise.

Hence, tears of sorrow! ye unbidden guests,
    That on repentant error oft await ;
Lo ! faithful memory her pure source attests,
    Sadly—not hopeless—calm, not desolate.
Sweet flood of tears ! that yet through memory's
        vale
May flow awhile, or cease in season brief ;
On thy pure stream canorous hope shall sail,
    And drown in Lethe's wavelets every grief.

THE TALISMAN.

It was an early morning hour,
  As, waking on my lonely bed,
The sun's bright ray with mystic power
  O'er every sense its influence shed.
I could not sleep—I did not dream—
For fancy fill'd with life the beam.

Yes! smiling forms and memories came,
  And revell'd in the golden light ;
An echoed vow—a treasur'd name—
  Renew'd the hours that once were bright.
The crowding motes came thick and fast,
And seem'd to whisper of the past.

I gaz'd upon the sunny scene,
  And thought how sad, whilst life doth flow,
That doubt should cast its shade between
  Those vows of faith that youth doth know.
Still thickly-peopled was the ray—
Still yet more vivid and more gay.

Sweet tuneful words of loving truth,
　With tender tokens of the past ;
Hair—braided in its sunny youth—
　And missives—dear from first to last—
Yet more and more increased the motes
Those tokens and those lover's notes.

At last, I could not bear the light ;
　I rose, and drew the veiling blind,
When pass'd for ever from my sight
　Those things which leave no trace behind.
Yet sadness seem'd to spread around
　Its dead leaves on th' enchanted ground.

A gentle voice broke on my ear :
　" Why thus indulge each vain regret ?
" I came to check thy falling tear,
　" And bid thee falsehood's wiles forget.
" How wert thou left when wrapt in shade ?
" Where have those motes of sunshine stray'd ?

" I came not by mere fancy led,
　" My mission was of love to thee—
" Now that thy days of youth have fled,
　" And Time hath laid his hand on me.
" For thee I grew a magic flower
" In deepest shade, in secret bower.

" I rear'd this flower—to thee a spell—
  " No gift more rare—beyond all art ;
" 'Tis thine alone where'er I dwell
  " No other eyes have counterpart.
" No perfum'd locks from beauty's hair
" With this, my gift, shalt thou compare.

" It is a talisman to thee,
  " For though 'tis hidden from thy view—
" Than wallflower in adversity,
  " Or rose to beauty not more true,
" To prompt thy muse and guide thy song—
" To thee its emblems but belong.

" Would'st sing of love ?—a myrtle leaf—
  " It comes to tune the roundelay ;
" Chang'd to an aloe by thy grief,
  " It turns to balm and makes thee gay.
" Each fires thy muse in genial turn,
" But its perennial life is fern.

" 'Tis near thy fancy's rosy bowers,
  " 'Tis near thy heart and dear to joy ;
" It calls back youth's remember'd hours,
  " Which cares of life would fain destroy.
" Release it, then, and banish fears,
" No more thine eyes degrade by tears."

Then silence fell—I did obey,
   And sought my secret treasures rare ;
Worn near my heart, imprison'd lay
   A souvenir of pale brown hair.
I knew it well, and fondly prest
Life's latest offering to my breast.

For ever be thine influence shed
   O'er all my thoughts—o'er all my days—
And, garish light for ever fled,
   Shall yield to thy unfaltering rays.
Thus thou shalt be for ever dear,
My talisman !—my souvenir !

LINES

SUGGESTED BY SEEING A PRINT REPRESENTING A CHILD,
WHO, WHILST ON A RURAL RAMBLE, STOPS TO TIE HER
SHOE-STRING ; HER COMPANION HAVING GONE ON, SHE
CALLS TO HIM, "WAIT FOR ME !"

A fairy scene—a cloudless sky—
I see the child with bright blue eye,
Who halts to fix a tie, now free,
And calls on one, " O wait for me ! "
Back, borne on scented air, I hear
His merry laugh—his ringing cheer ;
But yet responsive answers he,
" I'll wait for thee ! I'll wait for thee ! "

Some few short spring and summer days
They speeded on their errant ways ;
Still oft she call'd in youthful glee,
" O wait for me ! O wait for me ! "

M

But Time had fix'd th' unerring date,
And bade reply the voice of fate,
E'en from afar—across the sea—
" I'll wait for thee! I'll wait for thee! "

O life that was! O dreamy sleep!
Too short for joy—too long to weep.
In sorrow, on her bended knee,
I hear her pray—" O wait for me! "
A voice upon the midnight air,
In spirit tones—in accents fair—
From starry paths of ecstacy,
Responds, e'en yet, " I wait for thee! "

THE PROTEST OF " C."

TO A LADY, WHO PROPOSED AS AN ANSWER TO AN INQUIRY
AFTER HER "COLD," TO OMIT THE LETTER "C" FROM
THE WORD, AS MORE DESCRIPTIVE OF HER COMPLAINT.

———

Commencing in candour—though truth I don't
 claim—
In complaint I am heard when attack'd is my
 name.
In " cold " I was born—in the middle of ice ;
To virtue unknown, I was brought up in vice ;
But enough 'tis to know that by day or by night
No Critic's two *eyes* can dispense with my sight ;
Then why should you deem me unworthy to name
The very same feeling the frigid but claim ?
And casting me *out* of, not *into* the cold,
Prefer a new title, and say it is " old."
But pr'ythee beware of a contest with me,
Lest mischief arise from rough treatment of " C."
Though some with indifference coldly may move,
True love, e'en if *old*, will its warmth ever prove ;

And though youth hath its "charm," yet none
   will deny
Its virtue lives only with me standing by.
Remove me—'tis gone, and the risk be your own,
For harm doth remain for which none can atone.
Then bear with me, lady—receive my fond call,
Contentment and comfort I offer to all;
And rest well assured, life a pleasure will be,
When each I've just mentioned doth flourish
    "*per se.*"

TO THE MEMORY OF

THE LATE EDWARD REDMAN, Esq.

If ever worth and truth did sweetly blend,
    Here lies the heart that did possess them well;
Reader, had'st thou the hope to find a friend
    Who in such virtues purely did excel—
Mourn then with us this truthful worthy man,
    And end thy hope just where our griefs began.

How great our woe, who knew and lov'd him well,
    No words can measure, and no time efface;
Our gain was all his life—O who shall tell!
    A worth no time to come shall e'er replace.
Then, pilgrim-stranger, thus our sorrows flow
    With hope departed, sad our mutual lot;
Though unbereav'd, yet doth Death's cruel blow
    Confirm thy first great loss—to know him not.

TO A LADY ON HER BIRTHDAY,

WITH MY FIRST BOOK OF POEMS.

A birthday gift, from friendship's hand!
 Auspicious may it prove to be—
Some musings in that dreamy land—
 The poet's realm of ecstasy.
Some joyous revels 'midst the flowers
 That fancy's summer ever rears.
Some thoughts that tell of wintry hours
 That mark life's heritage of tears.

Yes! such they are; and as this day
 Recalls thy first of earthly care,
So hope would bid my muse essay
 A birthday in thy thoughts to share.
And that my book, not scorn'd, but read,
 On many a birthday yet may show
Its welcome flowers—its leaves not dead—
 Though bleak Novembers come and go.

TO A LADY,

WITH AN ENVELOPE SHE HAD SENT THROUGH THE POST
UNSTAMPED.

Dear doubting friend, pray here behold
The proof of what you have been told,
How that a postman brought to me
A letter full of loyalty,
And yet with outward form so strange,
His wit at once foresaw some *change*.

He saw me lay the missive by,
And said, whilst casting kindly eye,
(For fear the change betoken'd pain),
For twopence he would call again.
And then, half soothingly, he said,
"That letter, sir, doth want *a head*."

He went—I open'd and enjoy'd—
(By what small fears we're oft annoy'd!)
The letter was as good as gold,
The heart's pure dictates to enfold;
Such genial missives nought can cramp,
And *bear inside*, at least, *their stamp*.

The man return'd—I knew he would ;
I said, as wistfully he stood,
" That letter was not frank'd, I find."
He only then got half my mind,
For it was plain that he could see
It had been *frank* enough to me.

Nor heeded I his letter'd thought—
Though many bright ones hath he brought—
A worthy fellow he appears,
A pilgrim on our paths for years ;
Nor stumbles he, I fearless say,
When *trifles are put in his way.*

So down I threw a shilling good,
Again with *thoughts of change* he stood ;
But waiting not to hear him thank,
I said, " That change is worth a franc."
He took—the hint, he saw my whim,
The change alone affected him.

TO A LADY ON HER BIRTHDAY.

Again the year renews its joy,
  Again the spring is laughing near,
And songsters of the grove employ
  Their heavenly gift in numbers clear ;
To welcome each returning grace,
  Each record nature loves to bring—
May not the poet now retrace
  Thy natal day of fairest spring ?

How sweetly guarded yon fair moon,
  That sails upon its azure sea,
And seems to pale her light too soon,
  Whilst lov'd and worshipp'd tenderly.
Like things of joy those golden spheres
  Attendant seem to watch and gaze,
And yield the lustre that endears
  The memoried light of bygone days.

O then, my friend, may beauteous prime
    Attend thee yet in many a spring;
Thy virtuous heart shall conquer Time,
    And check the swiftness of his wing.
May many a birthday o'er again
    Still see thee happy in thy years,
Thy lov'd ones be thy starry train,
    Thy worlds of joy!—thy golden spheres!

ON PRESENTING A LADY WITH HER FIRST SPECTACLES.

Yes! sure it is that print grows small,
　Or lights are troublesome and queer ;
Good writers now adopt a scrawl,
　Or else the note is held too near.

Is it a dark conspiracy
　That shrouds the tale we wish to read ?
For though the page we well can see,
　Some dancing imps the eyes mislead.

It matters little though we prove
　Bad print, or light, or scrawling friend ;
Or farther from the eyes remove
　The note we scarcely comprehend.

But lo! by the optician's skill,
　We gifted are with " second sight ;"
Occulted powers for good or ill
　Come with the new discover'd light.

So with clairvoyants we'll agree—
    In this we surely all believe—
That if by " second sight " we see,
    Transparent " mediums " can't deceive.

So, lady, take the profferr'd aid,
    And use it as thou hast a mind ;
Perchance aside it may be laid
    When thou wouldst be *a little blind.*

As when we trace 'midst blots and smears
    What we would gladly never know ;—
An unkind missive fraught with tears
    The magic glass might well forego.

Or if my lays offend thine eye
    By dulness or defective line,
'Twere well to pass them gently by,
    Nor use too much that light of thine.

Then may its gentle aid impart
    Perennial pleasures—sweet employ,
Lov'd pages still delight thy heart
    With smallest type—with largest joy.

LINES

ON WITNESSING A PICTURE BEING PAINTED BY MR. W. M. WATSON, REPRESENTING A VIEW FROM THE DRAWING-ROOM WINDOW OF MRS. GURNELL'S HOUSE AT WIMBLEDON.

———

Whilst standing at the window-frame
I watch'd the painter's careful gaze;
Sweet summer with her children came—
A rosy group of laughing days.
Slowly beneath her mystic wand
They rose to grace the charming scene,
And to the artist's tracing hand
Gave sweet assent—the summer queen.
Her smile restor'd the bygone bloom,
But fearing yet some evil sway,
His work to guard from grief and gloom,
She bade one faithful watcher stay.

Then on the colours sunlight stream'd,
Forth sprang the flow'rets everywhere;
The beauteous landscape only seem'd
To live for her whose home was there.

I gaz'd and wonder'd, for the year
  Had brown'd the harvest with its store,
And many a leaf was crisp and sere
  That lay about the garden-door.
Though on the outer fields there came
  This sign of change 'neath autumn's wiles,
Within, sweet summer, e'er the same,
  Bestow'd the magic of her smiles.

So now, whene'er we lingering gaze,
  The guardian of her chosen prize—
Lest Time should send despoiling days—
  Stands watchful there with loving eyes,
Attendant, should a cloud o'erspread
  The picture or the gazer's brow—
O'er all the scene sweet smiles to shed,
  And every heart with love endow.
How like this work is Gurnell's mind,
  Though Time should mar the prospect fair;
Who seeks her genial heart shall find
  Summer's attendant daughter there.

THE SEARCH.

Extract from a Letter to the Author from the Countess T——,
acknowledging the perusal of some " Lines on Presenting a Lady
with her First Spectacles."

*   *   *   *

"The lady must have been very much pleased. I think you
could make some lines on a lady who always loses her spectacles,
and is constantly running after them, though she is absolutely
blind without them ; so just try your poetic spirit, for that lady
is myself."

What art thou seeking, lady dear ?
So earnest in thy searching gaze,
In every nook—now far, now near—
In silent and mysterious ways.

O yes ! perchance thy truant keys
Have wander'd, heedless of their trust,
And now thy placid heart displease,
Detaining what thou would'st adjust.

Or it may be thy needed purse
    (Close to thy hand) evades thine eye,
Holds back what thou would'st fain disburse,
    And revels in disloyalty.

Thou say'st I incorrectly guess,
    Nor keys nor purse thy search employ,
But missing glasses, that will bless
    Thy vision with its pristine joy.

How sweet to think—whilst soon bereft
    Of valued friend to guide the way—
Our search will find one true friend left
    To light the evening of our day.

Yet let me twine a mystic wreath,
    And show my guesses somewhat right;
A purse is but a case or sheath
    That often holds a wondrous light.

For well we know how clearer far
    Some eyes will see 'neath golden beams,
How dense and dark *some* senses are
    Until a golden medium gleams.

And keys—they are a magic power,
  Without them oft are hopes denied,
And if mislaid one little hour,
  What darkness reigns on all beside!

'Tis *not thy* purse—what it may hold
  Would shed no light for thee to heed;
For well thou know'st, with nought *but* gold
  Our lives would be but dark indeed.

But to thy keys—my other guess—
  Thy glasses well compar'd may be,
To unlock riches, and to dress
  Thy mind in all its purity.

So to thy sight the glasses are
  The keys to open treasures bright,
To show thee many a hopeful star
  Upon the dusky robe of night.

To show thee what thy lingering gaze
  Without their aid would faintly prize,
And gild the sunset of thy days
  With joys that meet thy searching eyes.

N

Now thou hast found them, and regain'd
   Thy hold on pleasures of the sight,
The mentor muse is not restrain'd,
   But bids thee treat such friends aright.

Nor cast aside the kindly ray
   That shines from humble mediums free;
When dark, like cottage windows, they
   May mark thy path, and comfort thee.

But with thy faithful friends at hand,
   Nor careless thrown in sombre shade,
Thy wish shall be a sweet command,
   By all who love thee well obey'd.

Then shall thy search through life but prove,
   Like this, rewarded by success;
Whene'er thou seekest light or love,
   Thy search attendant both shall bless.

TO A LADY ON HER BIRTHDAY,

AND ACKNOWLEDGING THE RECEIPT OF "A SPRIG OF JESSA-
MINE GATHERED FROM A PLACE OF LOVED RECOLLECTIONS
LONG AGO."

This morn propitious,—let my muse essay
  A little flow'ret of the past to sing,
And cheerful hail the one returning day
  That doth with true accord its presence bring.

It lies before me—Flora's kindly sign
  Of winning gentleness and genial smiles ;
In life its odour, like a breath divine,
  Wafts summer to the heart, and time beguiles.

Gather'd and treasur'd, like the joys of yore,
  Till the returning kindred bloom again ;
So doth this day return in love once more,
  To show that time tries genial hearts in vain.

Sweet jessamine ! I love thy olden name !
  How dear thy sisterhood in bygone hours !
When on the air their scented missives came
  To bid us to the festival of flowers.

When o'er the porch and round the lattice
    stream'd
Thy galaxy of stars with odorous air,
Set in a lovely firmament, they seem'd
    Like angel eyes in watchful beauty there.

So, lov'd of memory ! thou remind'st me too,
    Now thou'rt brought forth upon this natal
    day,
How well thou bearest testimony true
    That sunny hours are not for ever May.

Old Father Time hath smiles for all the year ;
    'Tis now November, yet he trips along ;
To truthful hearts he gives his genial cheer,
    And welcomes e'en December with a song.

Thus then, my jessamine, and thou, my friend,
    On this remember'd morn be one in heart ;
This sleeping flower on memory shall attend,
    Till a sweet birthday wakes its counterpart.

Now 'tis *thy* turn, my friend, to wake to joy ;
    This is *thy* birthday, let thy heart be gay,
And thou from flowers shall draw some lov'd
    employ
    When *their* sweet birthdays usher in the May.

TO A YOUNG FRIEND,

AFTER AN ESTRANGEMENT OF SEVERAL MONTHS.

I take thy hand, and feel 'tis given
 Regretful of the time estrang'd ;
The tears with which thy heart hath striven
 Attest the old regard unchang'd.
And now my thoughts recur to thee,
For memory's child thou art to me.

Thou bring'st at times before my eyes
 The semblance of the lov'd and gone ;
Whilst fancy lingers and supplies
 The doubtful point in face or tone.
Thus, oft absorb'd, I've gaz'd on thee
In memory's sad, sad reverie.

Thou art not she—yet soft and low,
 Like hers, thy voice recalls the tone,
When, in thy childhood long ago,
 I heard it but from one alone—
Who stole like daybreak on my sight,
 With morn too gay—with noon too bright.

No more I go where memory leads ;
   Yet sometimes, when I see thy face,
I think of distant lanes and meads,
   And many an olden pleasant place ;
And fancy furtively recurs
To looks of thine recalling hers.

Perchance some eyes may fail to see
   The semblanc'd features I recall,
And wayward wanderings charge on me,
   Because thou own'st not one and all.
Let them gainsay, like flowers or trees
Whose aspects vary in degrees.

But I will, with a pure regard,
   See yet in thine the face of old ;
May brightest hours be thy reward,
   For dark ones come—estrang'd and cold ;
Nor e'er by thee be this forgot :—
Truth's tears are sweet—disown them not.

Thus none will blame me if I seek
   To bring again departed years,
Nor blush shall mantle on thy cheek,
   Because I mingle smiles and tears.
'Tis she ! when sorrow bendeth me,
If memory's moonlight shines—'tis thee !

MY WIFE'S DEATH.

DECEMBER 8TH, 1871, IN HER 54TH YEAR.

Thus, as the husbandman in autumn yields
His seed-corn to the furrows of the soil,
And thinks of days to come, and waving fields
That yet shall bless the promise of his toil ;
Or valued flower—its life in gladness shed—
Whose bulb in earth he stores for future bloom,
Awhile, in hope surrendered to the dead,
And all that faith can gather from the tomb.

Or when the sun—with summer nearly gone—
Shines forth with bright and e'en refulgent ray,
The heart in memory's sunlight gazes on,
And claims a hopeful and protracted day.
But lo ! from western skies untimely sent,
Dense clouds arise in early afternoon,
Which, scudding swiftly o'er the firmament,
Clothe the lov'd landscape in the night too soon.

Floweret of memory! thus I lay thee by,
   Thus do I hope for harvest field in store;
Sun of my morning! clouded in the sky,
   'Tis night—but shall not be for evermore.
Thou yet shalt live, where, in perennial bower,
   Bloom all the virtues lent to earth awhile;
Thou yet shalt shine where clouds can never lower
   To cast the shadow of an earthly guile.

Methinks I see, on that drear wintry morn
   When sunk thy life—when darken'd was thy
     beam,
Thy spirit rising—to the skies upborne,
   And lov'd ones waiting on thy vanish'd dream.
Yes! spirit voices hail thy welcome home;
   And as they tell of bygone earthly hours,
Lo! from the village grave four dear ones come,*
And bear thee onward to celestial bowers.

Thy sire, with loving welcome, opens wide
   The gate that ushers thee to golden joys;
See! hand-in-hand await thee, side by side,
   Our long-lost cherubs—thy three baby-boys.

---

* In the churchyard of Merton, Surrey, are the graves of our three children and my wife's father.—*See Note, page* 132.

Yes! all thou lov'dst in the days of yore
In joy attend thee to thy blest retreat;
Travellers, who went thy journey long before,
Greet thee—as only shall the faithful greet.

O star of hope! I gaze upon thy skies
Full oft, and fancy thou art watching now;
No tears bedew the brightness of thine eyes,
No brooding sorrow bends thy tranquil brow.
And time a little while may dally yet
Ere I shall gaze in spirit-life on thee;
Then may it be—earth's sun for ever set—
Thy loving hands shall ope the gate for me.

EPITAPH ON HER TOMB.

(IN HIGHGATE CEMETERY.)

Belov'd by all, a faithful course she kept;
Vice knew her not—in silence slander slept;
Truthful to all, she gave to varying years
Joy's genial smiles and sorrow's tender tears.

EPITAPH ON MY GRAND-DAUGHTER.

(IN ABNEY PARK CEMETERY.)

———

As shines the star, though noontide splendours
    hide
Its holy beam from earth's enraptur'd gaze,
So thou, dear love-light, though beatified,
    Affection hails thee through life's lingering days. *

See page 161.)

EPITAPH ON MY WIFE'S MOTHER.

(IN ABNEY PARK CEMETERY.)

———

Now sinks the beam that memory endears—
    Light of life's misty heritage of tears !
Whose rays protracted, waning in the west,
    Gilded life's clouds and glorified her rest.

(See page 156)

LINES

ON RECEIVING SOME SNOWDROPS IN A KIND LETTER OF
CONDOLENCE.

How many poets tune their lays
To snowdrops in the wintry days,
And touch the heart with mystic chords
Set to the tenderness of words;
When nature's death-like form appears
In icicles—like frozen tears,
Which, 'midst the requiem for the dead,
Were fix'd whilst yet profusely shed.

At once the floweret—timid maid!—
Receives the poet's serenade,
And songs of hope full soon are heard,
Though silent yet is every bird;
Because, though winter holds in thrall
The darken'd landscape like a pall,
Yet there the floweret snow-clad lives,
And mystic spells and blessings gives.

In twin-like form I here can trace
Sweet consolation's tender grace ;
In words her missive breathes of rest,
Bearing her floweret on her breast;
To calm the heart opprest with woe,
In sorrow's shade and wintry snow,
She sweetly sends a missive fair,
And folds her floral emblem there.

AGED "TWO."

TO A LADY, BORN MARCH 22ND, 1870.

———

Most thoughtless lady! pray attend;
   For as thou canst not read the time,
Let then a very loving friend
   A *reason* give for sending *rhyme*.
This day recalls the passing thought
   That e'er to us thyself endears,
By thy vagaries we are taught
   The mysteries of earlier years.

No learning thine content we rest,
   Nor hurry what we wish to teach;
Already broken words attest
   Thou'rt studying *now* the "*parts of speech.*"
Through all last year, with all its care,
   Thou hadst of love full quite thy due;
Now envious Time—*and brother there*—
   Demand of love enough for "*two.*"

Well! we can find it; and if years
   Go on like those just swiftly flown,
Time will bring nought but what endears
   All that belonged to " *one* " alone.
This plural year—the first to thee—
   Proves what we all may plainly view;
In varying stages age we see,
   And even thou art *aged*—" two."

O may it be!   Time, bring anon—
   Another heart, thine—only thine—
Pulsating in sweet unison
   To true chords strung by love divine.
For ever *then*, *one* heart, *one* life,
   When joined in holy bond so true,
Thy husband, with his loving wife,
   Be ever ONE, and never " TWO."

TO MY FIRST GRANDSON.

Thou art a little man ; so tell me, pray,
   What is thy world thou'rt striving so to see,
As, looking upward to the wond'rous day,
   Thou see'st two orbs peer tenderly o'er thee ?

So peer'd such orbs o'er sire and grandsire too ;
   The loving eyes of mother banish fears ;
They shine, whilst life holds place, for ever true,
   And varying only with their misty tears.

Thou art a little man ; then shout and bawl—
   'Tis but forerunner of the future days ;
Should years to come upon thy being fall,
   Thou'lt find how empty shouters bawl for praise.

Striving and struggling with thy tiny powers,
   Thou'rt but rehearsing, in thy cot, the plan
Which petty heroes, in life's later hours,
   Perform with pomp—to hide the little man.

But let thy grandsire hope (though to his eyes
   The vision come not,) this be thy career :
A youth of health—a heart without disguise—
   A virtuous courage that disdains all fear.

A manhood honest, frank and generous too—
  Calm, when conceited tyranny would vex;
With love unbounded for the good and true—
  Contempt for hypocrites, of either sex.

For strength mistaken, violence assumes
  A ready rudeness manhood truly loathes;
As a bad fire good fuel wastes in fumes,
  So a coarse fellow dons deceptive clothes.

Then may thy life be valued by the age
  That claims thy friendship and that owns thy
        worth;
Youth's vigour need not shun the poet's page,
  Nor culture spurn the attributes of earth.

Firm as a rock, when canting knaves appear—
  (As weakness deeming gentle bearing shown)
Unmov'd by flattery or the ready tear,
  Too oft put forth by deep deceit alone.

Thus healthy, wise, and kind and pure,
  Firm in thy courage knavery to scan,
Though *little* now, thy manhood shall endure,
  And thy best title be —"a gentleman."

ON THE MARRIAGE

OF

MR. STEPHEN T. PLUMMER,

WINE AND SPIRIT MERCHANT,

WITH MISS CLAY,

(SEPT. 19TH, 1872).

———

When rash Prometheus shap'd with earthy clods
A human form, and scandalized the gods,
To give it life he stole from heaven the fire,
And saw completed his profane desire.

Unlike Prometheus, lonely Stephen sigh'd
For heavenly grace to earthly form allied ;
At Bacchus' shrine the suppliant votary knelt—
('Twas whisper'd he with various spirits dealt)—
And pray'd the god to grant this boon divine
To crown his bliss—dispenser of the wine.
Bacchus, in genial mood, proclaim'd his want—
" My ivy fades ! my berries too are scant ;
" Behold ! the gods anticipate thy need,
" And earth, with life endow'd, shall be thy meed."

'Twas done ; and now, on this auspicious day,
Come forth celestial graces, cloth'd in *Clay* !

O

THE NEW YEAR.

—

Father Phœbus, tell me, pray,
    Why mortals only mark thy ruling,
When thou dost publish on this day
    Some new books clean for future schooling?

Thou goest round thy swift career,
    Thou makest furrows on thy track,
And send'st the harvest of each year,
    As promis'd by thy almanack.

When spring doth clothe the freshen'd fields,
    When summer tunes the insect's horn,
When wealthy autumn treasure yields,
    Or winter comes, on darkness borne—

Alike thou shinest; but thy sway
    Is hail'd with rapture, when on high,
Through Leo thou dost urge the day,
    With wingéd steeds in golden sky.

Thy progress noted in thy might—
   No progress mark'd in thy decline ;
And as thy rays recede from sight,
   Man's moody thoughts too oft repine,

So with this world—this thing of space
   Do myriad ages pass away,
And scarcely leave historic trace
   Of progress onward to decay.

But, Phœbus, thou'st seen ages die,
   And seen the glories of their sway ;
Their histories fables now supply,
   And progress questions, " Where are they ?"

Yet every age looks back with scorn
   Upon the poor benighted past,
And only sees a little morn
   To deem that noons for ever last.

Thus every age in which man lives
   Doth claim its own supremacy,
Nor sees His hand the means who gives,
   Proportion'd to necessity.

And as the unit of the whole
  The individual man appears ;
His wants, and comforts, and control
  But vary with the sum of years.

How shall we urge how sad their lot
  Who liv'd in dreary days of yore,
When many a science knew them not,
  Now trite—though needful to our store ?

Poor grovelling wretches, thinly spread !
  No brilliant gaslight in their dream !
They must have perish'd in the shade,
  Or doubtless died for lack of steam !

Doth progress now put all things right ,
  Nor hear we now of horrid crimes,
Nor strangling robbers lurk at night,
  In these enlightened present times ?

But, Phœbus, though I own I feel
  All partial to these modern days,
Suspicion I will not conceal—
  My mind's misgiving but betrays.

O! it were better could we learn
　From progress, or whate'er it be,
Some wiser system to discern
　The foes who menace liberty.

Shall dull monotony prevail,
　And new years but repeat the old?
Save changes, numbers but entail—
　Shall Time no purer state unfold?

The same self-worship rule the heart;
　Conceit, as ever, rampant be;
Shall labour shirk its honor'd part;
　Shall idle brawlers revel free?

It cannot rest that common sense
　Will long remain deceiv'd or blind,
Nor fail to see the weak pretence
　That lurks the demagogue behind.

Labour from capital estrang'd!
　Who but the worthless fatten then!
Who rave between them thus derang'd!
　Those who are neither gods nor men.

Hail, then, free trade! if it may be
 The rule of life by which to hold;
Duties and rights thus truly free
 Make labour's worth the par of gold.

So shall the worthless rant and rave,
 And all their little thunders roll;
Whilst merit, rising from its grave,
 Claims the first place on labour's scroll.

If progress mean but numbers' needs,
 Culture, if not to virtue nice,
Falling like rain on flowers and weeds,
 May bring forth scientific vice.

Doubtless our boasts may pass away—
 Our transient excellence be nought—
Our wondrous speed seem but delay
 To those who come with after thought.

Yes! it may be when Time and I
 Have closed the volume of the past,
The wants of progress may descry
 More wonders from its storehouse vast.

How strange to think it may be said,
  We, beings of an unripe time,
With muddling steam our only aid,
  Could never fly from clime to clime.

But, on the wings of wind, set forth
  (Mere routine in an age to come,)
From east or west, from south or north,
  Electric travellers journey home.

Who, when their usual day be o'er,
  Sing of the sorrows by us borne,
Some wit, with tables in a roar,
  Shall laugh our railway speed to scorn.

So, Phœbus, I am loth to hear
  Murmurs against thy magic sway ;
Thy progress lasts our little year—
  We see thy works and their decay.

We see thee with thy pristine grace,
  The same returning power divine ;
Our kind renew'd, we find our place,
  And thou alike on all wilt shine.

Cast then thy beams upon the heart—
　Teach us to feel a nobler fate ;
Nor fear to play life's worthy part,
　But kindly hours anticipate.

So shall we calmly view the time
　In equal pleasures pass away,
Each heart, with hopes and thoughts sublime,
　Begin a new year every day.

THE TYPIAD.

———

A COLLOQUY WITH MY CRITIC-FRIEND AND PRINTER,

JOHN SUCH.

———

Come sit thee down, my welcome friend,
And if we cannot things amend,
Let us our usual meal partake,
With just one glass for memory's sake.
Our common rule hath little chance,
The usual score—the usual range,
But we have one sure guarantee
That bars us from satiety ;—
Our ever varied converse makes
The fancied banquet each partakes.
Spreads o'er the board its viands rare,
And paints luxurious dishes there.

And then the illusive hour divine,
Bids us behold its dreamy wine,
And in the simples of the glass.
We see the priests of Bacchus pass ;

In fancy hear the votive strain
That bids us raise our cups again.
But not the wine-cup's sunny glow
Can yield the pleasure that we know,
When with our humble goblet fill'd—
With genial blendings—not unskill'd,
In converse, fancied paths are trod,
Ne'er painted by the rosy god ;—
'Tis ours to prize the minutes rare
Which wingéd Time doth grudging spare.

Perhaps 'twere well, as many a time
Thy thought hath qualified my rhyme,
My muse should own the little fact,
And feel the better for the act :—
This done, I cannot now resist
A little talk, so pr'y thee list,
And if my theme be dull and slow—
One thing for certain, well I know,
Thy ruthless friendship will " know why,"
And rate me soundly, by-and-bye.
What matter then ?—we're neither boys,—
Disparity too oft destroys
The valued truths that age imparts
To listening youth, who hears and smarts.
When precious lore is harshly given,
And far away kind influence driven ;

So, when I speak thou'lt listen fair,
And with my testy humour bear,
And I, when thou perchance may seem
A wakeful watcher o'er a dream,
And seeing some fantastic shape,
Which from the dreamer may escape,
Thou shak'st me well without pretence,
To bring me back to clearer sense,
Shall blame thee not, though I complain,
The waking hath been all in vain ;
That still across my fancy steals
The ecstacy the dream reveals ;
And though thy reasoning may be plain,
I revel in the dream again.

Thus as we give and take our words,
Each to the other oft accords
The pleasure of a thought exprest
In phrase that seems to please the best,
But yet no mentor he appears—
For both are stricken so in years—
As well pretend, each one of us,—
Is Chesterfield *redivivus.*

So now, my friend, I'll tell my theme,
And mark thee—'tis not now a dream,

I wish to *dress in print* again—
(Nay! put not on that look of pain),
But take the comfort to thy heart,
The blame be mine—nor bear a part,
Lest thou should'st seem to crafty scribes,
A mark for their puissant jibes,
Which killed poor Pope—a warning sad—
Despite his dreadful Dunciad.
So, Byron to oblivion fell—
As bards and Scotch reviewers *tell*—
How many pilgrims on the way
They slew in that chivalrous day.
I dare not mention, for 'tis plain
That Samson's bone may slay again ;
So let me baulk their vicious ends
And be content to print for friends.

I see a smile comes o'er thy face,
At least thou'rt sav'd from sad disgrace,
And thou can'st seek the critics now,
Nor bear a mark upon thy brow ;—
That brand which stamp'd the first of crimes
Long ere the rhymer murder'd rhymes,
Say, that thy brother lives, is true,
And thou hast been his keeper too.

So, " print for friends," well, why surmise
That friends are not to criticise ;
That some punctilious worthy friend
May not propose some lines to mend ;
Or that a whisper round may go,
That useless 'tis your faults to show,
And him, as friend, alone you view,
Who praises faults to flatter you.
Truly well put, but there again,
I think you somewhat overstrain ;—
He is no friend, who flatters e'er,
Not poets only this must share—
One golden rule through life we own,
But not to poets only known ;
Deceit too often flatters men,
Guiltless at least of poet's pen ;
Needless to name such weak pretence,
To those of worldly common sense ;
And sure I am, no friend of mine
Would flatter, though he lov'd each line,
Nor yet withold his warm assent,
That I had given an hour's content.

Thus having clear'd the doubtful ground
On which such undergrowth is found,
I fain would frankly tell my friend
Me none can flatter—none offend ;

And but for reasons which we know
Are fair enough as customs go ;
I would not fear to launch a boat
That on the stream of love should float,
If truth alone impell'd the tide,
Nor special craft e'er sail'd beside ;
Still if I seem to breathe a tone
That doth to disappointment own,
Me pray forgive—for I declare
The " craft " hath borne me true and fair,
And many a wet sheet in the breeze
Hath flutter'd to my reveries,
Unknown to pilot or to mate
But, thrown aboard by hand of fate
On sunny seas when once afloat,
Rose to the breeze, nor swamp'd the boat.

But may I tell the secret charm
That dar'd e'en foes to do me harm ;
Or, worse than foes, the " faint praise " friends,
Whose balance always downward tends ;
And I am sure you will decide
That I did right to curb my pride
And take my critics in a bunch
To form a pleasant bowl of punch.
For well you know (I teach you nought)
How true that spell you love is wrought

" One sour "—" two sweet "—or I am wrong
Next says the recipe " three strong,"
" Four weak " comes in to blend the whole
And mingle the occulted bowl.

O PUNCH immortal !—thou whose power
Hath wrought the fate of many an hour,
Whose potent baton is the ban
That falls upon the charlatan.
What was the influence wrought the spell
Thy hunch-back monarch wields so well—
The bowl divine ! the glorious blend
Of many a cynic—many a friend,
Who from the treasures of his wit,
When drain'd thy bowl, replenish'd it;
Bitter and sweet its spiriting
And mingled with th' Aonian spring.

So did I learn in earlier days,
When all my hope was gentle praise,
When churlish frowns were really pain,
Nor did I know folks frown'd for gain,
Or veer'd to smiles as chang'd the wind
And scarce a fault would deign to find,
When pass'd the proper channel through
(As kissing goes by favor too)

I own'd the justice of the frown,
Which keeps the interloper down ;
So then to mix the bowl I plann'd
I sought the recipe at hand ;
For sour and sweet, and strong and weak,
I had not very far to seek.
One critic of my early days
Who never, never vouchsaf'd praise,
Unlucky very, 'twas for me,
He read " the bird sang from the tree "
In fury he look'd up and cried
" What bird ! what tree ! must be supplied,
" Or who can tell what 'tis you mean. '
" Or even if the tree were green."
Enough ! to see his awful frown—
I bottled him, and cork'd him down.
" I have the sour at least said I
Whene'er to blend my bowl I try.

Then next an editorial wight
With bardish friend came on my sight,
Who sang in lovely woman's praise,
And very worthy were his lays.
All would have been quite well I own
If he had but been left alone,
But oh ! his patron simper'd well
When I one faulty rhyme would tell ;

Gravely assur'd me poetry
Did not consist in rhyme "*per se*,"
And that the " dimples " of his fair
Rhym'd well with " sprinkles " anywhere.
I felt abash'd—I only meant
To bar a weak rhyme from consent,
So that the sweetness of their love
Should never detrimental prove ;
But as I only play'd the deuce,
I bottled them for future use.
Thus sour and sweet I having got,
The strong and weak—the cold and hot,
Come ever ready to my share
From many an editorial chair.

Now as my bowl I often blend
And sit in converse with a friend,
Though my ingredients tax my skill,
Each striving to assert its will,
They find I rate them all alike,
Lest one predominant should strike ;
In due proportion to the aim,
Content I mingle praise and blame.

Then place your chairs my critics all,
In friendship let your accents fall,

Fill from my bowl the subtle blend,
And such concordance shall attend,
That sour, or sweet, or weak, or strong,
Which to each temper may belong,
Shall find its special hue doth pass,
Lost in the colour of the glass.

Thus then, dear Typo, I have done
(You think perhaps my tether run)
Thou hast been patient as a friend
My critic too—with much to mend.
" The world "—condens'd in this shall be—
A friend is all the " world " to me ;
With such a " world " as this 'tis plain
Critic and friend ne'er need be twain.
Unbiass'd eye our faults to show
The *Critic* only then we know ;—
Unswerving truth, with kindly praise
The *friend* then smiles upon our lays,
And leaves to time, the verdict true,
That overmasters all review.
If on my muse kind fate attend
Such be my Critic—and my friend.